BLOODY FOOL FOR LOVE

BLOODY FOOL FOR LOVE

A SPIKE PREQUEL

BY WILLIAM RITTER

HYPERION

Los Angeles   New York

First Edition, August 2022
10 9 8 7 6 5 4 3 2 1
FAC-004510-22049
Printed in the United States of America

This book is set in Adobe Caslon Pro/Adobe
Designed by Phil Buchanan

Library of Congress Cataloging-in-Publication Data
Names: Ritter, William, 1984– author.
Title: Bloody fool for love : a Spike novel / by William Ritter.
Description: First edition. • Los Angeles ; New York : Hyperion, 2022. • Series:
Buffy prequel series ; book 1 • Audience: Ages 14–18. • Audience: Grades 10–12. •
Summary: "Spike plans an epic heist against a ruthless gang of undead criminals in
1900s London in order to get back the one he loves." —Provided by publisher.
Identifiers: LCCN 2021007544 • ISBN 9781368071987 (hardcover) •
ISBN 9781368073929 (ebook)
Subjects: CYAC: Vampires—Fiction. • Demonology—Fiction. • Criminals—
Fiction. • London (England)—History—1800-1950—Fiction. •
Great Britain—History—Edward VII, 1901-1910—Fiction.
Classification: LCC PZ7.R516 Bl 2022 • DDC [Fic]—dc23
LC record available at https://lccn.loc.gov/2021007544

Reinforced binding

Visit www.HyperionTeens.com

For Katrina, the loveliest of all the monsters.

CHAPTER ONE

CHINA, 1900.

The fires of Beijing danced in Drusilla's eyes as she watched the city fade into the distance. Soon the raging rebellion was no more than an orange glow on the horizon, drifting gently into darkness, yet still she watched it. And Spike watched those eyes.

It wasn't about the rebellion. Spike knew Drusilla well enough to know she would not miss those crowded streets or the splendid violence erupting across them. Pools of blood and broken glass were easy enough to come by, after all. Much as she had savored the scent of fear and the sweet sounds of screams on the breeze, her eyes would not be watching for the chaos or the carnage as it shrank away behind their carriage. They would be watching for *him*.

Angelus.

Angelus had come back to them. After two long years without a word, he had come back, and their broken bloodsucking family had been made whole. Darla had Angelus, Drusilla had

1

Spike—they were the fanged four once more, and the wide world lay at their feet. But then, just as quickly as he had come, the bastard was gone again.

Darla was the most betrayed. She had scarcely spoken since he fled, except to inform them coldly of his treachery. Darla had sired Angelus, and for a century and a half, they had been each other's most intimate allies. Even after he had sired Drusilla and Drusilla, in turn, had sired Spike—Angelus and Darla had still had something special. But then the fool had gotten himself saddled with a soul. He was a vampire with a conscience now, and so was lost to them, perhaps forever. Drusilla had taken the news in numb silence. It was the silence that rankled Spike most of all. But what was there to say?

If the rebellion had struck China like a righteous and harmonious fist, then Angelus had struck the family like a coward's dagger—in and out in a flash, all the damage done before the pain had time to set in.

It was setting in now.

Spike leaned his chin on his hands and scowled as the carriage rocked. Twenty-four hours ago, he had been in the middle of the best night of his afterlife. He had sunk his fangs into a slayer's throat. Drusilla had licked the girl's blood from his fingertips and gasped in excitement at his touch. For one glorious night, Spike had been everything that she needed, and for a fleeting moment, all had been right with the wicked world. And then the moment was over.

Drusilla's eyes remained glazed, locked on the dim horizon as the carriage bounced along, and Spike was left with a familiar ache. Even at his best, he would never be enough.

The feeling settled thickly inside him like the soggy half of a biscuit slumping into a cup of tea. It bobbed up and down in his chest, turning everything that had been so glorious before into miserable, sodden mush.

Spike took a deep breath. His undead lungs might not need the air, but he still needed the moment. No. He was more than enough.

His days of whimpering in back alleys were over. Spike might have left London as another common blood rat, but he was returning a verified villain, a slayer killer, a god among vampires. Trembling Watchers would whisper his name to slayers-in-training for generations to come—and Drusilla would be happy. Things were going to be better. Just wait.

London was ahead of them, and this time it was going to be glorious.

ENGLAND, 1901,

London was underwhelming. At least, *under* London was underwhelming.

What the dusty basement lacked in amenities, it more than made up for in stench. The smell—like rotten ham with hints of cheap perfume—had been content to sulk in the back room for the first week or two, but lately it had begun to stretch its legs, loitering moodily in the parlor and even pushing its way into the bedrooms at the most inconvenient times. It was a dogged stench, a stench with dreams and ambitions.

Spike sighed.

There were no windows down here—not that any of the current residents would have been inclined to open them if there had been. Mismatched bricks along the outer walls belied places where openings used to be, now just memories written in the masonry. This whole floor had once looked out onto the bustling streets of London. It had known the touch of sunlight and the scent of fresh air. In those days, it had been carpeted with expensive rugs and furnished with finely upholstered settees and plum armchairs. The only furniture that now remained in the dimly lit chambers were the pieces too ragged and embarrassing for their former owners to allow them into the light where anyone might see them. They had been left behind to be bricked in, and then the streets had risen around them, and the world had forgotten the place even existed.

That was all ages ago, of course—well before the various lines of London's underground railway had burrowed under the city. The basement's previous tenants had been long dead by the time the railway's work crews accidentally knocked a hole in the eastern wall. The new tenants—who had found their way in through that damaged wall—were technically long dead, too. But they were a much more active sort of dead.

They were not nearly active *enough* for Spike's taste, though. He sighed again, only louder.

"What's the matter?" asked Darla, not looking up from the pages of her book. She was lounging on a moth-eaten divan in the corner. "Is the poet warrior feeling uninspired?"

"I am feeling inspired," Spike said, "to drive a stake through my sodding temple if I have to stay cooped up again all night. We've been back for weeks, and we've barely left the nest. Is it any wonder poor Dru is getting so antsy?" He slouched in his chair, drumming his fingers on the battered table. Drusilla sat across from

4

him, shuffling a deck of cards and humming tunelessly to herself.

"Drusilla is fine." Darla turned another page, slowly.

Spike noted the title, set in a gaudy red script on a yellow cover. He scoffed. "Bad enough you brought that rubbish into the house," he whinged. "But do you have to actually *read* it?"

"It's interesting," said Darla. "This Stoker fellow got a lot of things right."

"Hurrah," Spike grunted without enthusiasm. "Trade secrets revealed."

"Don't be jealous. Not everyone can be Dracula."

"Not everybody *wants* to be. I'm not jealous of that puffed-up plonker." Spike gave a snort and slid his chair back with a squeak. "I'm going out."

"Now?" said Darla, allowing her gaze to creep up over the top of the book. "What for? It's only an hour to sunrise."

Spike pushed his hair out of his face. "To get someone to eat."

Darla scowled. "You still haven't even finished that iceman you brought home last week."

"The iceman's gone off," said Spike. "He's all peaky. I'm gonna find a nice lamplighter or something. Might stop by the old Shady Shop on the way home. Don't worry. I'll be quick about it."

"You haven't got any money for the Shady Shop," said Darla. "You spent the last of it getting Drusilla that overpriced dress."

Spike sneered. He *did* remember the dress. He had forgotten about the money.

"I still don't know why you didn't just drain some strumpet behind the dance hall and take *hers*, like a normal vampire," Darla muttered.

"Because Drusilla wanted *that* one," said Spike. "And Drusilla deserves to get nice things from time to time that haven't been worn by mutilated murder victims."

Drusilla glanced up from her cards. "Aww. My Spike is always so sweet," she said. Her eyes crinkled with a smile.

"Frankly, I think the mutilated murder victims are half the fun." Darla shrugged. "They give an outfit a bit of history."

"Ugh. I could do with a lot less history," Spike said. "History packs too much baggage. More interested in the future. Our future." His eyes flicked to Drusilla. For a moment, he seemed to forget what he was saying. His chest rose and fell as he watched her shuffle the battered cards—but then he shook himself back to the present. "And in my immediate future, I'm going out," he declared, "before I start bashing my head into the wall just to feel something."

Darla shook her head. "Fine. As long as you don't forget that we have an appointment to see Lord Ruthven at the guild tomorrow." She went back to her book.

"Wait, Spike." Drusilla spread the deck out on the table in front of her. "I'm going to read your cards before you go. Angelus likes me to keep in practice."

Spike's mouth twitched, but he nodded and put on a smile. "All right, Dru. Just a quick one. Go ahead."

"Your current condition is"—Drusilla laid a card on the table—"the four of cups." On the card, a boy sat beneath a tree with a collection of goblets around him.

"Bollocks to the cups," muttered Spike under his breath. "My current condition is *stuck in a rotting basement.*"

"Discontent, my sweet one. It means you're unsatisfied."

"The tarot picked up on that, huh?"

"Don't be smart," she chided. "Got to lean into it."

"Lean into it?" Spike shrugged. "Wouldn't mind leaning into four or five cups—maybe a whole bottle."

"Your greatest obstacle is"—Drusilla ignored him and laid another card atop the first—"the knight of wands."

Spike leaned over to peek at the card. "He looks like he's on fire. Who's that bloke supposed to be, then? Some sort of wizard? I could fight a wizard."

"The knight of wands is hastiness. Frustration. Rash action."

"Hmm." Spike grimaced. "I *could* fight a wizard."

"She's right," Darla called from the divan. "You don't think. You never take a moment to plan things out, you simply rush in and sow chaos everywhere you go."

"I *do* think," answered Spike. "It's just that I happen to do some of my best thinking in the middle of the chaos, thanks."

"And then we're stuck picking up the pieces for you," Darla added. "It's not cute, Spike. It's selfish. And reckless."

Behind them, Drusilla laid out another few cards and tutted softly to herself.

"When have you ever had to pick up my pieces?" Spike said, turning in his chair.

Darla crossed her arms. "Stockholm? Frankfurt?"

"Those don't count."

"Saint Petersburg?"

"Again with Saint sodding Petersburg! That was as much his fault as it was mine!"

"How about Wiltshire, then?" snapped Darla. "Last month?"

Spike hesitated. "What was wrong with Wiltshire?"

"You mean besides you making an unholy spectacle of yourself?"

"I was *celebrating*! It was a *party*."

"You knocked a stone off Stonehenge."

"It was a *good* party," said Spike. "Come on. It was our home-coming! We were back from China—I had just slain a slayer! The humans can put their big stupid rock back on top of the other rocks. No harm done."

"No harm? You broke the lintel and set a Squamus loose in the world."

"Did I?" Spike frowned. "Wait. Was that before or after we ate those druids, because I was hallucinating pretty heavily for a bit there. Druids always have the best mushrooms. What's a Squamus, anyway?"

"Pestilence demon? Several tusks? Covered in sticky scales?"

"Oh! That guy!" Spike brightened. "He was fun! Best New Year's I've had in decades. Nineteen hundred and one, Darla—a whole new century. What's the big deal? It's not like the scaly bas-tard caused a scene or anything."

Darla finally closed the book and set it on the table beside her. "He killed the queen of England. It made the front page of liter-ally every paper across the country."

"He gave her a nudge!" Spike countered. "Come on. Victoria was eighty-one. She was basically dead already, and it still took him three weeks to get the job done. Toothy scrub was good fun at charades, but not the most efficient monster in the mix, if we're being honest."

"Do you ever take anything seriously?"

"Life's not about waiting for the carotid artery to stop hemor-rhaging, Darla. It's about learning to dance in the spray."

"Ugh." She rolled her eyes.

"What? Would you rather I was more like your precious Angelus?" Spike said.

"Don't," growled Darla.

"Seven of swords . . ." Drusilla murmured behind them.

"Your perfect Angel," Spike continued. "Always seriously sadistic and sadistically serious. He never stopped to smell the corpses. Never threw a punch he didn't know would land. Never made a single move he didn't ponder for days first."

"That's enough," Darla hissed.

"Really makes you wonder"—Spike cocked his head at her—"how long he was planning to abandon us before he finally up and did it. Twice."

Darla was on her feet in an instant. She narrowed her eyes at Spike, fingers clenching and unclenching, before she spun around and stormed out of the room.

Spike ground his teeth.

"Fool," said Drusilla, airily laying down another card.

"She started it."

"The fool means new beginnings. Risks. Spontaneity." The image on the tarot card showed an old-fashioned jester standing on a cliff overlooking the ocean.

"Right," said Spike. "That's me, then. Bloody fool." He leaned his elbows on the table. "So, what's our future hold, princess? And don't say death. I always get death—a bit on the nose for a vampire."

Drusilla dealt three more cards. "A partnership. Broken trust. Deception."

"That'd be the past," Spike grunted. "How's it all work out in the end?"

Drusilla flipped the final card. It showed a tall brick tower in ruins, buffeted by a storm, fire dancing from the walls and smoke pouring from its windows as bodies plummeted toward the rocks below.

Spike eyed it. "That one looks cheery."

"Destruction," Drusilla said, scowling.

Spike pursed his lips but then put on a reassuring grin. "Everyone else's, Dru. We're not the tower—we're the flames."

Drusilla smiled. "That's right, my sweet. The four of us against the world."

Spike's jaw set. "Three of us," he corrected.

Drusilla made no indication that she had heard him as she swept the cards back into her deck, humming softly to herself again.

"Right. Well then. Back in a bit, love," said Spike. He plucked his frock coat from the broken rack beside the crack in the wall. "I'll see if I can't pick you up something nice."

CHAPTER TWO

The streets of London glistened in the lamplight as Spike emerged aboveground. All around him, the air was thick with the familiar bouquet of coal fires and horse dung and gritty, rotten, raw humanity. He had missed London. China had been a lark, sure—they hadn't even needed to hide the bodies with all the excitement of the Boxer Rebellion raging around them—but China had never felt like home. Neither had Russia or Germany or any of the other stops along their wicked world tour. Nowhere on earth was London but London.

Spike found his feet carrying him along the old, accustomed paths. Even the frosty breezes of this damp January night were like familiar voices, whispering through the narrow lanes, welcoming him back. He knew these towering buildings with their stately gables and soot-darkened brickwork; they had loomed over him his entire childhood, their wrought-iron spires stabbing the sky and their chimneys belching black smoke. There were streets like these all over London, whole neighborhoods bordered by brick giants who all but blocked out the sun even in the middle of the day, bathing their neighborhoods in blessed pools of darkness. Darker still were the myriad nooks and crannies that splintered off the main roads like spiderwebs. Those dim corners used to intimidate him when he had been timid William Pratt—but William Pratt was twenty years dead. For Spike, the darkness was an old friend. It was a friend that stank of spilled beer and might or might not attempt to mug him now and again—but a friend, nonetheless.

His hand slid absently into the pocket of his coat as he shuffled along the sidewalk, and after a few paces, he realized that his fingers had wrapped themselves around a stiff piece of folded paper. The ticket. He fought the urge to crumple the thing into a tight ball and toss it into a gutter. Being rid of it would not make it weigh any less heavily on his mind, but that didn't stop the impulse. He released his grip and withdrew his hand, instead.

The clink of a bottle and a faint sniffling caught his ear, and Spike changed course to slide silently toward the sound. He crept down a nearby alleyway. If he strained his ears, he could make out a heartbeat thrumming invitingly just ahead. Excellent. A quick back-alley murder always helped him take his mind off his troubles. Spike took his time, savoring the stealthy prelude. The approach was almost better than the kill. It was like opening a present. What delectable surprise awaited at the other end of the cobblestones? Would it run? Scream? Put up a halfway-decent fight? He approached noiselessly, keeping to the shadows.

A single dirty gaslight illuminated the scene from above as he emerged through a crumbling brick archway. At the other end of the alley, a woman sat slumped against the wall behind a rubbish bin. A bottle—gin by the smell of it—rolled loosely in her grip. It plinked like a gentle chime against the cobblestones when she moved. She wore a plain dress with the sleeves pushed up to her elbows. Her arms were skinny, and her head hung low. She appeared to have a bright green pencil tucked behind one ear, but it might as easily have been a leaf.

She was a scrap of a thing, barely more than a snack, and she looked ready to topple over at any moment even without Spike's help. He shrugged. He would have preferred some light sparring or a quick run to work up an appetite, but he wasn't about to turn his nose up on a well-marinated meal. He stepped into the feeble light, and the woman lifted her chin.

Dark lines ran down her cheeks. She sniffed and wiped her eyes. She didn't even look startled to see a strange man looming over her. Spike tried looming *harder*, but to no effect. The woman just looked . . . defeated.

Sodding hell. She was taking the fun right out of it.

"Hullo there," Spike tried.

"I haven't got any money," she said, slurring her words only slightly. "Unless you're here to murder me horribly. Are you here to murder me horribly? Like . . . erm . . . whossname? Jack the thingy?"

"Ripper?"

"Thass the one."

"Amateur," said Spike. "Sloppy. And shorter than you'd think."

"Who's short?" The woman swayed.

"Don't worry about it," said Spike. "You look like hell, do you know that? Plus damp. It's really ruining the moment for me."

The woman sniffed wetly and wiped her nose with the back of her hand—or she tried to, but she chose the hand that was holding the neck of the bottle and ended up pouring gin all over her dress instead. "Lord above," she mumbled. "Sorry." She let the bottle drop and tried to brush herself off, ineffectually. "Sorry. Sorry."

Spike rolled his eyes. He should just do it now and put the wet mess out of her misery. He took half a step closer. The girl's bottom lip was quivering.

"Hell," he muttered. "Hold on. I think I've got a handkerchief somewhere. Here." He passed her a wrinkled pocket square.

"Th-thank you," she said meekly. She rocked slightly as she reached for it, and slumped back down hard once she had it.

"Oh," she said, blinking at the cloth. "Is this . . . blood?"

"Mm? Oh. Yeah," said Spike. "It's not mine, if that helps. Came with the coat."

"The kerchief did—or the blood?"

"Both." He leaned against the bricks and eyed her, like a wolf watching a kitten, while the woman dabbed at her dress. He *was* going to finish the thing. He was. It was just that she had thrown off his rhythm, and now the timing felt all wrong. Besides, good presentation is half the meal, and this one was a sodden disaster. He would let her clean herself up a bit, first.

"Was it a bloke?" he said when the silence had begun to feel awkward.

The woman sniffed.

"It was, wasn't it?" said Spike. "Men are pigs, right? Well. A bit like pigs. Not as chewy. More coppery. What were we saying?"

"It wasn't a man," she said.

"No?" Spike tilted his head. "A lady? Not judging."

The woman looked as if she was trying very hard to contain her emotions for several seconds, and then a dam burst. "Mary Shelley was only nineteen when she wrote *Frankenstein*!" she blurted, and she was sobbing.

"Oh." Spike blinked. "Oh? I think I might have lost the plot," he said.

"Th-th-thass what th-they said, too!" she whimpered. She reached into the pocket of her dress and produced a damp, crumpled page.

Spike gingerly unfolded the soggy paper. He could only make out every other word. "*Miss Eriksson*," he read. "That's you, then? *Per your recent . . . not interested . . . beneath the sensibilities of our . . .*" He squinted at the page. "Is this a rejection letter?"

"I'm twenty-three, and I h-haven't published *anything*. I'm a *failure*."

Spike rolled his eyes, but he sat down on an old crate beside the pathetic woman. He let the letter dangle wetly from his thumb and forefinger as he picked up the bottle of gin. "Used to do a bit of writing myself."

"Yeh?" The woman sniffled. "Were you any good?"

"Honestly?" He took a swig. "Bloody awful. Nobody liked it. Not even my own . . ." He hesitated and cleared his throat. "Nobody. I met the love of my life in an alley like this one, as it happens, blubbering about a rejection of my own. Been with her ever since."

"Did you keep writing?"

Spike pushed himself off the wall and paced in front of her. "I took a . . . different path," he said. "But if I hadn't poured my heart and soul into it back then—if I hadn't got that brutal rejection—I wouldn't be the man I am today."

Miss Eriksson did not look buoyed.

"Look, the point is, you can't let a bunch of arrogant philistines tell you that you're not good enough for them. What do they know? What does"—Spike squinted at the smeared ink—"*J. P. Bockspurn* know?"

Miss Eriksson's lip quavered into a smile so weak it collapsed under its own weight almost as soon as it had formed. "What if it just wasn't any good?"

"Maybe it *wasn't*." Spike shrugged. "Maybe it was rubbish! Still can't let a bunch of stuffed shirts look down their noses at you. To hell with rejection, and to hell with the damned fool doing the rejecting. Leave him in the past. You don't need him. He was only ever gonna hold you back anyway, the way he looked at you with such disdain, treated you like you were nothing. That smug look on his pretty-boy face." Spike's expression darkened.

"Erm. Are we still talking about Mr. Bockspurn?" asked Miss Eriksson.

Spike blinked down at her. "Focus on the future, that's what I'm saying. Keep writing. When someone tries to get in your way, you kick them in the knackers and keep going to spite the bastards."

Miss Eriksson giggled. "Thank you," she said. "I am glad you didn't murder me horribly."

"Yeah." Spike sighed. "About that . . ."

Spike was disappointed with himself as he cut across Curtain Road. A couple of months ago, he had been dancing over the corpse of a ruddy slayer, and now he was sulking through Shoreditch like a gutter rat with a curfew. Miss Eriksson had not left enough gin in the bottle to soften the blow.

He *could* have killed her. He would have, if he had wanted to.

This was *not* an Angelus situation. Spike had *not* lost his edge. He had *not* gone soft. He was still at the top of his game.

The flagstones along the sidewalk glittered with a light frost. Lights were flickering on in a few nearby windows as early risers began preparing for the day. Half an hour until sunrise, but Spike wasn't worried. It was fine—the Shady Shop was only a few blocks away. He could still find something to make Drusilla smile and be back underground before the first sunbeams carved their way through the morning fog and melted away the ice.

"Oh, for heaven's sake, Wesley!" Up ahead, a man in an expensive overcoat was yelling at a boy on the sidewalk. "I told you to have the horses sorted and ready! I am supposed to be in Wembley by eight in the morning, you useless whelp!"

"Sorry, Mr. Bockspurn!" young Wesley called, already halfway down the street toward the stable houses. "I'll have the horses hitched and ready straightaway, sir!"

The man harrumphed and crossed his arms to wait.

Spike slowed his pace. "Did that kid just call you *Bockspurn*?" he said aloud.

"Mm?" the man grunted, sparing Spike an unimpressed glance. "What's it to you?"

"You wouldn't be J. P. Bockspurn, would you?" Spike asked.

"What do you want? I don't give handouts, boy."

"But you do publish books?"

The man looked Spike up and down. "Not interested."

"That's what you told Miss Eriksson, too. Along with a few other things. She showed me the note."

"Lord above." Mr. Bockspurn let out a long-suffering sigh. "This is why I never accept submissions from women. I'm *not* sorry, if that's what you're looking for. I meant every word of it! You can tell that insufferable saddle-goose that both she and the rest of the literary community would be better for it if she never put pen to paper again! The world does not need any more fantastical fluff or vulgar horror. I publish *serious literature*, sir."

A vein on the man's temple pulsed. Even through the bluster of the man's voice, Spike could hear the steady thrum of a heartbeat.

"Have you read that manuscript of hers?" Mr. Bockspurn was still ranting. "Three-hundred-odd pages about some ridiculous monster? Nobody wants to read that!"

A smile was edging its way up Spike's mouth like a blade sliding out of a sheath. "Who doesn't like a good monster, Mr. Bockspurn?"

Mr. Bockspurn was craning his neck to watch for the return of his servant boy, but young Wesley was nowhere in sight. The street was empty, but for the two of them. "Hmph," he grunted. "That sort of drivel might appease the ignorant masses, but mindless penny dreadfuls are, quite frankly, *beneath me*."

If Mr. Bockspurn had been paying attention, he might have noticed Spike's brow had grown heavier and his eyes had sunk into dark shadows. He might also have noticed a wicked set of fangs revealing themselves behind Spike's parting lips. He might have read the writing on the wall.

Spike had *not* lost his edge.

When Wesley finally arrived with the carriage several minutes later, it was to find a curious stain on the sidewalk where his master had been. The horses stamped and chuffed impatiently. They never did make the trip to Wembley, after all.

The clerk at the Shady Shop slid out from the back room, noticed the body slumped over Spike's shoulder, and scowled. "No food or drink in here," he said. "You're dripping all over the— Whoa. Wait a minute. Spike? Is that you?"

"The one and only, Gus." He shifted the weight of J. P. Bockspurn's remains awkwardly on his back. He shouldn't have done it—not in the middle of such a public thoroughfare so close to morning—and now he was stuck lugging his leftovers around. Maybe Darla wasn't entirely off the mark about the merits of the whole *think before you act* concept.

"I heard you was back in town!" Gus leaned on the counter. "Is it true what they're sayin'? About China?"

Spike raised an eyebrow. "Depends on what they're saying."

"That you took on a bona fide slayer in single combat." Gus looked left and right, then leaned in closer to whisper conspiratorially, "And *won*."

Spike's lips turned up in a smirk. "Do I look like I lost?"

"Blimey. Everyone's sayin' you're nigh unbeatable in a fight now. Top tier. I told 'em I knew you back when."

Spike made a strained effort to look nonchalant in the face of the news. "Is that what they're saying?" he replied. "Top tier? Fancy that."

"Sure enough. I bet you could charge twice what you used to in the old sinister-services industry. Oh! Talking of which, Mad McElroy's putting together a team to pull off a good old-fashioned slice and heist over in Sussex soon. Should be a proper bloodbath. Right up your alley. If you like, I could give you his address."

"No." Spike straightened. "You don't go from taking down a slayer to taking orders from the likes of Mad McElroy. I've seen that guy eat an entire tin of beets in one sitting."

"Well, he's a bit odd, sure, but—"

"The *entire* tin, Gus. Tin and all. He didn't open it. He just sort of tipped his head back like a seagull and made horrible gagging sounds until it went down."

"Okay. Maybe not Mad McElroy. Harry Hammond? He's a respectable old vampire. Pays a fair rate, too."

"I'm nobody's hired goon. Not anymore."

Gus shrugged. "I suppose you are in a whole new league these days. There's a few sayin' you'd even give ol' Dracula a run for his money now."

"Ugh." The smile dropped from Spike's face. "I'd have to give that bastard a run for *my* money, first. Tosser owes me eleven pounds."

"You know him?" said Gus. "Did you hear they wrote a book about him while you was gone? I think I've even got a copy or two in stock still."

Spike's mouth tightened. "I heard about the book."

"Of course you did," said Gus. "I suppose nearly everyone's heard about it. Could hardly walk through Camden Town without seeing it in the shopwindows for a while there."

Spike simmered.

"Made the count even more famous than Lord Ruthven," Gus added. "Cor. Can you imagine? Think they'll ever write a book about you?"

"Why are we talking about books?" Spike burst out, nearly dropping the body. "Nobody reads books!"

"All right. All right." Gus relented. "Was there somethin' in particular you were lookin' for today? I've got a nice set of vintage plague masks, just came in last week. Authentic, too. Stink of death all over 'em. Robes to match, if you're interested."

"Nothing like that." Spike shifted what was left of Mr. Bockspurn on his shoulder. "I'm looking for something nice for my girl, Gus. You still carry those fancy black parasols you used to have? The ones with a blade in the handle and lacy bits around the edge?"

"Oh, sure. Always popular, those." Gus bustled over and fetched one from a bin at the end of the counter, then trundled back to set it in front of Spike. "Same blackout fabric as always, but the latest style has a hint o' red in the lining, see? Real classy."

Spike nodded. "Nice touch."

"Anything else?"

Spike considered. "Don't suppose you've got anything that can make someone get over the past and look forward?"

"I know a witch who could do you up a quick memory-purge spell. Only takes a pinch of Lethe's Bramble, and I got plenty of that in stock. Perfect remedy for erasing a thing or two that you don't want the missus to remember." He winked.

"No good." Spike sighed. "The part of her past she needs to move on from is bit more than a few squabbles or a naughty night out with the boys. It's sort of—her entire afterlife."

"Ah. You want something more like the Relic of Saint Agabus," said Gus.

"Relic of who?"

"Agabus. He was this biblical fortune-teller. Kind of a big deal, I guess, because somebody went to the trouble of saving a piece of him. Just being near the thing is supposed to heighten your foresight, help you see what is and what could be. Plus, there's stories about it giving a few people crystal-clear visions of the future."

Spike looked impressed. "Dru likes prophecies *and* body parts. Don't suppose you've got one of those tucked away in the back?"

Gus shook his head. "There's only the one, far as I know. Finger, I think. Deathwok Clan got their hands on it for a while, but then there was a whole kerfuffle with some Blackhearth agents, and it wound up back with the church in the end."

"Of course it did." Spike grimaced. "Never mind—forget I asked. Just the parasol."

"That's three shillings."

"Right," Spike said. And then he remembered. "About that. Think you might let me have it on the house this time? You know. As a token of your admiration for a top-tier slayer killer?"

Gus drew a breath in through his teeth. "Spike, my friend," he said. "You know you're more'n welcome here. But I can't go giving away the merchandise. Bad for business. Shady Shop's barely staying open as it is, what with the latest protection fees to the demons and whatnot. Razor-thin margins."

"*Bad for business?* Ugh. Fine. Here." Spike shrugged the corpse off his shoulder. It hit the tile floor with a heavy slap. "How about you take whatever this tosser had in his pockets."

"Spike."

"What? He looks like a posh bloke. He's good for it." He gave Bockspurn a nudge with his foot. "Probably."

Gus sighed and slid out from behind the counter to kneel beside the body. "You know this isn't how it works. If I want to keep the lamps lit and the collection demons off my back, I need cash, not corpses. You can't— Whoop. Hang on. Bloody hell. He's got over a pound on him. Yeah, that'll do. Be wanting some change, then? Or shall I consider it a credit for the next time you're in the market for one of my nefarious little knickknacks?"

"Sure. Credit me." Spike plucked the parasol off the counter and gave it a satisfied twirl. "You'll take care of my leftovers, yeah?"

"Dispose of the body, you mean? What kind of an establishment do you think this is?" Gus shook his head and tutted. "Of course we'll take care of the body. Got a bin in the basement. Bloke from the guild picks up the scraps every Thursday. I know a guy at a teaching hospital who pays decent money for organs and skulls and the like, too, if they're not too ripe. They're hard up for raw materials lately. Good old-fashioned back-alley murders are in a steep decline around here. Sad state of affairs."

"Well then," said Spike. "Happy to support the local economy. Looks like I'm good for business after all."

CHAPTER THREE

The sky had lightened to a pale purple gray when Spike finally dropped into the sewers beneath Hackney. He only needed to navigate a few blocks of these mucky passages before this route would take him to the railway tunnels, and then it was a straight shot back to home sweet hovel.

He took care not to let the brand-new parasol brush against the walls. There was a walkway of sorts on either side of the reeking underground river, but it was narrow and often slick. Sewers under London could be surprisingly stately passageways, but they were still sewers. He could hear the muffled clop of hooves and the rattle of carts as the city above him gradually awoke, and he found himself needing to duck under the occasional shaft of sunlight that came sneaking in through the overhead grates. He might have pushed it a bit too close for comfort—not that he would admit as much to Darla.

Ahead of him, just past a bend in the corridor, he heard steps. Ugh. Toshers. Spike had learned early on not to bother with their lot—scrawny kids who scrounged through human waste for a few fallen coins and lost rings. He would rather go hungry than put his lips on a tosher's grubby neck. He waited, hoping the footsteps might veer off down a side tunnel, but the sound was growing louder, each step echoing in the grimy corridors.

The figure who came tromping around the bend was no scrawny kid; he was a man as broad as an ox and dressed too nicely to be hunting tosh. With a tweed flat cap pulled low over his eyes, the bloke nearly plowed straight into Spike before he realized he wasn't alone in the tunnel.

The lug was way out of Spike's weight class, but Spike was feeling ornery, and his more violent instincts kicked in before his brain could catch up. With the element of surprise on his side and the rush of fresh blood still coursing through him, he drove a hard left hook into the big guy's rib cage.

Spike's whole arm shuddered upon impact. A solid sucker punch from Spike should have been enough to break an average man in half—but this felt like hitting an oak tree with a tweed waistcoat wrapped around it.

Oof. Not human, then. Good to know. Spike shook his wrist.

The bruiser let out a startled grunt and threw a wild punch in return that could have knocked the teeth out of a rhino.

Spike managed to duck aside half a second before the blow landed, and the meaty fist glanced across his temple instead of pulverizing his whole skull. Whatever this creature was, it recovered with surprising speed for something the size of a land mass.

Spike's vision blurred, and he spun on his heel and stumbled backward.

The parasol slipped from his grip.

He rallied as quickly as he could, blinking rapidly in the gloom of the tunnel and willing his eyes back into focus. For a moment, two fuzzy images of the titan swam back and forth in his vision, both of them squaring their shoulders. Spike's eyes flicked downward.

"Wait!" Spike yelled before the bruiser advanced any closer.

The figure hesitated.

"Watch the parasol."

There was silence for a moment, and then an incredulous "Spike?" The voice was deep and gravelly, but also familiar.

Spike blinked. The man's features gradually came into focus. "Hammond? Harry Hammond?"

Hammond was a vampire Spike knew from his early days as a creature of the night. Everyone knew Hammond. He had been haunting the streets of London since back when Darla still had a heartbeat. And everyone liked Hammond. Or at least, the ones who survived liked him. The vampire was built like a stack of bricks, and he could snap tombstones in half with his bare hands—but the last time Spike had parted ways with Hammond, it had been with a hearty laugh and a slap on the back after sharing a pint or two of an unfortunate street sweeper.

Hammond's overlarge muscles relaxed, and he plodded forward, stooping to pick up Drusilla's parasol as he did. It looked like a toy in his hands. He handed it to Spike, scratching the stubble on his chin between a pair of bushy muttonchops. "Heard you was back in town. Been an age, mate. Sorry about the face. Caught me by surprise is all."

"You and me both." Spike took the parasol and wiped it off as best he could with the back of his sleeve. "You can't go jumping out around corners like that and not expect to get into a scrap. It's a good thing for you I didn't take your head off."

"It's a good thing for those pretty cheekbones of yours that you're still a quick dodge, you mean," said Hammond with a wink. "Thought you was one of Gunnar's boys with the way you came at me out of nowhere."

"Who?"

"Gunnar?" Hammond shook his head. "Devil almighty, Spike. You have missed a lot, haven't you. Gunnar's a demon. Real nasty one, too. Seventh circle. He runs the whole London underworld these days."

"So?" Spike massaged his sore temple. "Somebody has to, don't they? Crime's not gonna organize itself."

"Not like this. Trust me. I've been working the unseemly side of this town since there was still a Tudor on the throne, and I've never seen the likes."

"He's that bad?"

"Gunnar's crew have Old Smoke by the bollocks, and no mistake. The demon's toadies have marked all of London as their territory, and they been pissing on us local lowlifes to prove it. It ain't like it used ta be, Spike."

Spike shrugged. "It never is."

Hammond shook his head grimly. "Say, you wouldn't be looking for work, would you? Bleedin' demons have run off half my regular payroll, and either snatched or staked most of the rest. I got a job coming up could use more muscle. Big payoff. Heavy on the violence, like old times. What do you say?"

"You always did offer a fair rate, mate—Gus and I were just talking about you—but you couldn't afford me even if I was." Spike dusted an invisible bit of lint from his filthy frock coat. "Or haven't you heard? I'm a top-tier terror these days. Slayer killer."

"What I heard," said Hammond, "was that you and your pack are nesting in a moldy hole in the ground out by that new Central London line. Don't try to tell me you couldn't use a bit of ready bustle to improve your seedy environs."

Spike's brow furrowed. "My environs are exactly as seedy as I like them, thanks."

Hammond held out his palms in surrender. "Suit yerself. Just seems unequal to the likes of the famous fanged four."

Spike's eye twitched. "Fanged *three* these days," he corrected.

"Right, right. I did catch something about that, too," Hammond said. "Is that why you're so sour? I'm sure your old pal will come around in a decade or two."

"I'm not sour," snapped Spike. "And Angelus can piss right the hell off forever. I hope he bathes in holy water."

"Had a bit of a falling-out, eh?"

"That bastard. That absolute bloody bastard. Every time! It always had to be about him. If I was the moon to Dru's earth, then Angelus had to be the sweltering, sodding sun. You should've seen the way she used to look at him when he was brutalizing a victim—that thirsty look, like she wished it was her. I would *kill* for her to look at me like that. I *have* killed for it, in fact. Countless times. Never feels like enough."

"I dunno," said Hammond. "She always seemed mighty sweet on you from where I was standing."

Spike had picked up a head of steam and didn't seem to hear him. "He had a hundred-odd years on me to get a head start on his reign of terror, you know—built a name for himself before I was ever sired, the wanker. But I really put the fangs to the grindstone. I decided I was gonna make myself everything she could ever want and more. The biggest bad. And I did it, too! Drusilla tasted a slayer's blood on my lips and we danced in the fires of a rebellion, and for once, I was on top of the bloody world—but does that absolute mosquito of a monster let me have a single day to bask in my glory before making it all about himself again? Of course not!"

"Up and left?"

"Up and left!" Spike waggled the parasol. "Wouldn't even murder one little baby for Darla before he went."

"Rude."

"Right?" Spike huffed. "Good riddance."

"So? What're you gonna do, now that you're cock of the roost and you've got your lady love's undivided attention?"

Spike sighed heavily. His eyes wavered to the flimsy parasol in his hands. It suddenly seemed exceedingly inadequate.

Hammond coughed. "Well, I know rolling up your sleeves for old Harry Hammond may not be a job up to the caliber of a resident slayer killer with a lady to impress, but I'm operating out of the old Lang Building over in Shadwell if you change your mind in the next few days. Always room on the crew for a scrapper who don't mind getting his fangs bloody. Dru's welcome to come along, too. Make a date of it."

"Thanks, Harry. I'll think about it."

Hammond tipped his cap, and Spike gave him a parting nod and stepped aside to allow the boulder of a vampire to squeeze past. Heavy footfalls gradually faded into the distance as Hammond vanished into the shadowy tunnels.

Spike plodded on mutely through another quarter mile of sewer, the slap of his feet on the dank stones his only company until he reached the junction with the rail lines. There, he waited at the crack in the bricks for a long train of passenger cars to rumble past before hopping out into the Twopenny Tube. That's what they were calling it—the Twopenny Tube. The cheap seats. Mediocrity, even for the mediocre humans who clattered past by the hundreds to get to their mediocre jobs.

Spike's whole body felt heavy. He inspected the parasol in his hands. The silky black fabric had taken on a drab sheen on the side where it had landed, and the more he rubbed, the worse the stain seemed to get. He gave it an experimental sniff. It smelled like everything else down here, which was probably not a good sign. So much for nice things. Dejectedly, he tossed it into the shadows as he neared the broken wall of their humble abode. The basement was easy to miss if you didn't know it was there—just another pile of muddy rocks in the middle of a dank, dark tunnel. Hammond was right. This was *not* the second life that a top-tier terror deserved.

"Did you get me anything, dearest?" Drusilla sang as Spike slipped back into the hideaway. She had spread newspapers over the table and was squinting at them through a fat glass marble. The papers were a week old. One of them professed Queen Victoria was making a spirited recovery. Drusilla looked up dreamily from an article she had been reading upside down. "Darla said you wouldn't remember, but my Spike always gets me the nicest things, don't you?"

Spike winced. "Not this time, love." He tossed his coat onto the wobbly rack by the entrance. The hook snapped off under its meager weight, and it flumped onto the dirty floor. Spike willfully ignored it. "They didn't have anything good enough for you."

Drusilla's face melted into a scowl. "But you said you were going to."

"And I *will*," he insisted, sweeping close to her. "I'll get you such nice things. Nice clothes. Nice furniture to sit on in a nice house with a nice front door—maybe even a nice torture room in the basement with nice strong chains."

Drusilla drove a piercing stare into Spike, her face drawing so close to his he could have felt her breath, if she had been breathing. He leaned in, pressing his brow against hers. A moment later, her expression relaxed and she straightened. "Of course you will." She ran a hand lovingly along his neck. "That's my Spike."

Spike smiled and brushed a lock of hair behind Drusilla's ear. "You deserve better than these . . . *seedy environs*," he said. "And you'll get it, my love. I promise. Just you wait."

Looking only mildly unsatisfied, Drusilla made her way back to the table and dropped down in front of her newspapers. Spike's chest felt tight. Trudging up the narrow hallway, he pulled the stiff paper from his pocket and unfolded it. Simply holding the thing made his fingers feel clumsy and his arms go all leaden.

"What's that?"

Spike nearly dropped it. "Nothing."

Darla leaned on her bedroom doorframe and raised an eyebrow.

Spike glanced behind him and lowered his voice. "It's a ticket," he said at last. He held it out, and Darla took it. "I found it last night, looking for a pair of scissors for Dru. It was in a drawer with some scraps and a manky old bird skull."

Darla scowled. The ticket was for a single-person, one-way passage to Germany. It had been issued recently, but the date of departure was left open.

"She's planning to go looking for him," said Spike. "Without us."

"She told you that?"

"She didn't have to," said Spike. "And I didn't see any spare tickets in there for you or me. She's gonna leave us. I thought coming back to London would . . . I don't know—but clearly it *didn't*. If I don't find some way to help her get over Angelus and start feeling content with the likes of me, then I'm gonna lose her, Darla."

Darla pursed her lips and folded the ticket back into a tidy square. "You're being stupid," she said, but softly. "Drusilla isn't about to leave you. Not that she shouldn't. Frankly, I still don't understand what she saw in you in the first place."

"There's that supportive encouragement I was looking for."

Darla regarded Spike silently for a few moments. "You want to keep Drusilla? She's a seer. Give her something to *see*. If you want her to stop looking to the past, then give her a future to look forward to."

Spike knitted his brow.

"And don't worry about this." Darla tucked the ticket into her dress. "I wouldn't even mention it to Drusilla. A woman should always have a few options squirreled away to keep her from feeling trapped. You just worry about making yourself the *best* one."

After Spike had left, Darla closed her bedroom door and rested her back against it, her lips pursed. This was her own fault, of course. She had been careless—but how was she to know the twit would go snooping through that old broken vanity? Nobody else ever used the thing. She sighed. With any luck, Spike was the only one who'd seen the ticket. She wasn't ready for Drusilla to know.

She plucked the troublesome piece of paper back out of her dress and tucked it safely into her purse instead, nestling it alongside the letter with which it had arrived.

Soon.

Her throat felt tight. Soon, but not yet.

CHAPTER FOUR

Dripping pipes echoed through the tunnels as Darla slipped along the labyrinth beneath the city. At the junction, the tunnel widened. Pale limestone lined the corridor. Familiar territory. The chambers that housed the Order of Aurelius were not half a mile ahead. She felt a twinge of tightness in her chest.

The last time she trod this path, Angelus had been at her side—still a young vampire in those days, and as raw and wild as lightning. She had taken him to meet the Master and had carried what was left of him away afterward. First impressions had never been his strong suit.

Darla shook her head at the memory.

Her sire had warned her then that she and Angelus would not last forever. He had offered her a place at his side, a stable home, and grand ambitions to aspire toward—but Darla had chosen the wildfire that was Angelus instead. Of course she had gotten burned in the end. After all this time, the Master had been right.

There had been good years, to be sure. They had been the whirlwind, their little family. For a time, Darla had reveled in the swirling chaos that they caused and the desolation they had left in their wake. But every whirlwind must eventually dissipate. Now, in the settling dust and dying breezes, Darla was forced to face reality. Even the fiercest winds are without substance—dwindling to nothing, their momentum failing. The same chaos that had made a life with Angelus so exhilarating had also made it ephemeral. It was always going to end this way. The Master had seen what she could not.

His letter had arrived shortly after their return to London. Drusilla and Spike had been out fetching a fresh victim. Darla had not yet dared to wonder if the Master would even take her back when an acolyte of the Order, a vampire called Elita, arrived at the hovel. She had called Darla *sister*, bowed respectfully, and surrendered the envelope reverently.

Darla's eyes had widened upon seeing the Master's seal on the letter, and she had not blinked until she had read its contents twice.

The Master was presently abroad, the note explained, on perhaps the most important crusade of his immortal life: to open a dormant hellmouth and usher raw evil into the world. His loyalists had narrowed down a list of half a dozen possible locations from Kiev to California, starting with a derelict temple in Berlin. It would take time to check them all, but they would soon identify the most viable site and unlock a portal to the demonic realm—and with it, the true potential of the Archaeus bloodline.

Word had already reached the Master of Angelus's betrayal—of course it had. Without so much as a mention of Darla's poor choices, the Master had welcomed her back. He called the timing auspicious, in fact; she could finally put the error of her ways behind her and become a part of his grand, villainous plot as it ascended to its zenith.

Anticipating her enthusiasm to comply, he had paid for her passage in advance. All that remained was for her to join him in Berlin and reclaim her place in the Order. Also, his postscript urged, bring wine. German wine was like American blood. Palatable, but only just.

The light in the tunnel ahead fluttered, and Darla's nose twitched. "You can come out," she said. "I know you're there."

Elita stepped into what passed for light in the dim corridor, a feeble moonbeam trickling down through a high vent. Her hair hung in long black waves, and her dress was a red so rich and dark it nearly faded into the shadows. "Sister," she said, closing the gap between them. "I did not expect to see you again in London. You have been summoned, yet you still have not rejoined our Master?"

"I'm thinking about it," said Darla. "Have you been sent to make sure that I do?"

Elita shook her head. "If I had been, you would already be gone."

"That's good, then," said Darla. "For both of us."

Elita cocked her head. "Do you not wish to rejoin the Order?"

Darla hesitated. She was certainly ready for something more than penny-ante murders and meaningless mayhem. Returning to the Master at last? Opening a hellmouth? Reshaping the very world? That could get fun.

But what about Drusilla and Spike? If *Angelus* had been too arrogant to submit to the Master, then *Spike* was doomed. The Master would have the idiot's smirking head on a pike. Leave Spike behind, and Drusilla would be a lost cause as well. She would not abandon her pet for all the blood in Bristol.

"It's complicated," Darla answered. "I have responsibilities I must attend to first. What's your excuse?"

"I serve the Master here."

"Babysitting me?"

"No." Elita's eyes lit up, and her mouth twitched wickedly. "I pursue a worthier cause. Something in London has invoked the fury of an *Old One*."

Darla scowled. It was the Order's solemn purpose to serve and worship the most ancient of primordial demons under the Master's guidance. "Why do you sound excited about that?"

"It is written," said Elita, "that the stones shall tremble, the crown shall fall, and the blood of Archaeus shall become the salvation of Sorm."

"Yeah, well," said Darla. "It's also written that the eight o'clock to Shepherd's Bush will leave promptly on the hour, but that's hardly ever true, now is it?"

"The portents have already come to pass," Elita said, ignoring her. "On the eve of the new year. A mighty stone did fall from Stonehenge."

"Right. I wouldn't read too much into that. Could have been anything. Wind. Earthquake." She cleared her throat. "Some idiot who'd had a few too many druids."

"Now the mortal queen is dead," Elita continued, "and the mighty Sorm, the Old One whose slumber paints nightmares in the minds of men, has not been seen in months. I have been chosen to find him. I await my chance to prove our bloodline worthy."

"Block," said Darla.

"What?"

Without further warning, Darla swept the woman's leg with a

swift kick and drove a fist into her chest. Several bricks splintered as Elita's back hit the ground hard.

"Ow."

Darla stood back patiently and gave the acolyte time to gather her senses and sit up.

"You wish to fight me, sister? Very well, prepare for—"

"No," Darla interrupted coolly. "I don't. And trust me, neither do you. I was only curious. One of our bloodline is supposed to save an Old One? Maybe you? Why not? But you couldn't even stop little old *me* from dropping you like a spoiled corpse, so what exactly do you think that you're capable of taking on that an Old One couldn't handle on its own?"

The woman rose to her feet, scowling at Darla as she brushed off her skirts. "It is not for me to know—it is for me to be ready to do what I must when the time comes."

"Sure." Darla shrugged. "Good luck with that."

"Just as it is for *you* to rejoin the Master and experience the exquisite honor of helping him usher in a new era of evil for our kind."

"Right." Darla pursed her lips and nodded. "I will."

"And yet . . ."

"I *will*," Darla repeated.

"Then you are delaying the inevitable. Our Master is not known for his patience." She turned her back. "Good luck with *that*," she added as she disappeared into the darkness.

Darla bit her lip. It *was* inevitable. She could not put off closing the *whirlwind* chapter of her afterlife much longer. She would go soon enough, leaving Drusilla and Spike to their own uncertain fortunes. But not yet. They weren't ready to be alone in the wide world. The very moment the two of them were left to their own devices, Spike would almost certainly bring trouble crashing down on their heads. The fool could bury himself for all Darla cared—but she didn't trust him to dig Drusilla out of it on his own.

There were resources available to vampires who knew where to look for them. Darla had built up countless connections over the past three centuries—but Drusilla had barely been undead for forty years, and Spike for only half of that. They were practically babies. Darla needed to ensure that Drusilla was well connected to the right low-society vampires—that she would have someone to turn to when an angry mob started sharpening their stakes and lighting their torches.

Darla squared her jaw. The appointments had already been made. Drusilla might have been able to glimpse possible futures, but it was Darla who was going to deliver her a good one.

CHAPTER FIVE

Dust trickled from the rafters the following night as the eight o'clock to Liverpool rattled past. Spike brushed flakes of faded paint out of his hair and slammed a cupboard shut.

"Dru," he called over his shoulder. "Do you know where the oats are? I swear we had half a tin in here yesterday." He opened another cupboard. Empty, save for a dusty tea service with four chipped teacups.

"Yes, my love." Drusilla nodded, then scrunched up her face. "Wait. No? I'm not sure. I think I saw them last week—but it might have been tomorrow."

Spike's eye twitched involuntarily.

"I threw them out," said Darla, straightening her dress as she emerged from her room. "The rats kept getting into the cupboards. Why did you even bring home oats in the first place?"

Spike leaned both hands on the countertop with a heavy sigh.

"He likes the way they feel," answered Drusilla. "He mixes them up in the blood like a lumpy-bumpy bloody porridge. It's adorable."

Darla raised an eyebrow incredulously.

"What?" Spike said. "Sometimes I like a little texture when I'm eating."

Darla pinched the bridge of her nose. "I imagine this is what wild wolves would feel like if they had to watch their descendants becoming poodles." Darla shook her head. "Oh, I got rid of the iceman, by the way. I don't know why I'm the only one who ever clears out the leftovers around here."

"Whiskey for breakfast it is," said Spike. He pulled a half-empty bottle from the drawer and blew a spider out of a glass tumbler.

Darla rolled her eyes. "If you hurry up, we can grab a bite on the way there. London street urchins are always nice and tender this time of year."

"And if I *don't* hurry, I can do both," Spike said. "Hold on. On the way to where?"

"Please tell me you haven't forgotten our appointment with the guild. I've only reminded you about it every day for the past week."

"You can't expect me to remember things just because you say them out loud," said Spike. "Next you're gonna expect me to start *caring* about things, too."

"I remembered, Grandmother," Drusilla crooned.

"You need to stop calling me that," said Darla.

"Ugh. The guild." Spike poured the whiskey. "They're a bunch of nobby old plonkers. Claudia acts like she invented murder, and Count Orlok always smells like rotten cabbage."

"He doesn't," said Darla.

"Always."

Darla clenched her fists and looked to the ceiling as if imploring the family of beetles living in the molding to give her strength.

"I'm not arguing about this. We've been in town for nearly a month, and we still haven't declared status."

"And why should we?" said Spike. "So they can come asking for our help when the local werewolves get ornery? Or so they can tell us not to leave our corpses out by the curb on weekdays?"

"Your grasp of political etiquette remains as sharp as ever," said Darla. "This isn't some backwater town in America. The London Vampires' Guild look out for their own. They have connections. It pays to maintain a little decorum."

"We've always looked out for ourselves just fine."

"Having other vampires owing us a favor once in a while might be nice," said Darla. "Or wouldn't you like to know about upcoming opportunities? Nocturnal soirees? Real estate openings that don't smell like the sewers in the meat-packing district?"

Spike scowled and nodded grudgingly. "Fine. But I'm finishing my breakfast first. Most important meal of the day." His glass sloshed as he plopped down into the chair opposite Drusilla.

"I thought you *liked* fighting werewolves, Spike," said Drusilla. Her eyes drifted out of focus as she ran a fingernail gently along the lines of the old newspapers on the table. "Especially werewolves of London."

"I do." Spike cleared his throat. "But I prefer bashing hairy heads on my own terms. I'm not gonna play mindless muscle for some bureaucratic middleman. What's the point in killing a ruddy slayer if you still have to work for a living?"

"Will Angelus be coming with us, Grandmother?" Drusilla called over her shoulder. "He's been awfully quiet lately."

Darla and Spike exchanged a dark glance. "No, my dear," said Darla. "Only the three of us."

Spike took a deep, melancholy sip from the tumbler.

Drusilla lifted her chin and locked eyes with him. "Are you sad, my pet?"

He grimaced. "A bit four of cups, love. I'll come out on top, though, you'll see. Let me know if those fancy cards of yours get any better at telling me how to get there."

Across the floor, Darla pulled on her coat. "How to get *where*, exactly?" she said. "Will you be whisking Drusilla off to Milan next? Prague?"

"I think it's her turn to pick," said Spike. "Why?"

"It won't matter," said Darla. "You're never content in one place for long. Where are you actually hoping to end up?"

"Currently?" Spike answered. "The bottom of this glass. I think I can make it, too, if I get an early start." He tossed the remaining contents down his throat. As he brought it back to the table with a clack, Drusilla's hands clapped onto his. Spike blinked, startled.

Drusilla's gaze was a thousand miles away, and her grip held his fingers tight against the tumbler.

"Dru?"

Drusilla didn't answer. Slowly, the glass began to move, sliding smoothly over the crinkled paper, leaning left and pulling right, as if the whole table were some elaborate, messy Ouija board. Her eyes closed and her shoulders swayed slightly as the empty tumbler spun around and around in a narrowing spiral until it came to a rest at the center of the table.

After a moment's pause, her grip relaxed. She opened her eyes and leaned over to peer into the glass, her head tilting to one side.

"What do you see?" asked Spike.

"The future, I think," Drusilla breathed. "Made up of funny little words."

Spike leaned over the table to look, too. He wasn't sure what he expected. Tea leaves? Some swirling crystal vision playing out inside the dirty cup? He blinked. Warped slightly, and magnified by the bottom of the tumbler, the words from the wrinkled newsprint below it were clearly visible. Spike read aloud: ". . . *reliquary of Saint . . .*" His eyes widened.

He shoved the glass aside to get a better look at the article beneath it. *"Among the precious artifacts currently housed in the still-unfinished Westminster Cathedral,"* he read aloud, *"is the holy reliquary of Saint Agabus, a priceless vessel containing the left pinkie finger of the patron saint of fortune-tellers."*

His lips continued moving as he scanned the rest of the article, and his eyes began to sparkle as if he had just shaken a parcel on Christmas morning and felt a still-warm heart bumping about inside it.

"This is it!" He slapped the table. "It's the exact bloody thing!"

Darla peered over his shoulder. "A two-thousand-year-old finger?"

"Patron of fortune-tellers!" said Spike. "What do you think, Dru?"

"Is it for me?"

"The whole world is for you," said Spike. "But yes, that dusty old digit, specifically. Might help make your visions clearer, make it easier for you to focus on the—erm—right things. What do you say? You want it?"

Drusilla's lips were curling into a smile as Spike's infectious enthusiasm swept her up. She nodded. "Are you going to get it for me?"

Spike stood, rapping the table with his knuckles. "I've said it before and I'll say it again, if my princess wants a decrepit, severed piece of a dead man, she gets one." He swept around the table and took Drusilla's hand in his.

Across the room, Darla scowled darkly. "Spike . . ."

"You mean it?" Drusilla was beaming hopefully.

"It's a promise." Spike kissed her knuckles. "A *pinkie* promise."

"Spike," Darla repeated, more firmly.

Spike met her gaze. With a grumble, he tore himself away from Drusilla. "One moment, love."

"Drusilla, my dear, why don't you go fetch your coat and get ready," Darla suggested. "I need a brief word with our dear William the Bloody Idiot before we leave." She waited for him beside the crumbling hole in the wall.

Once they were alone, just outside the basement, Darla lowered her voice to a whisper. "You cannot keep saying things like that," she hissed.

"Like what?" Spike scowled. "That I'm gonna fetch an old relic? Watch me."

"You're delusional! Even if it is authentic, which it probably isn't, that thing is locked up in Westminster bloody Cathedral. Have you seen that place?"

"Heard about it. Went up while we were away, right? It's just another church."

"It's a church that makes your average church look like a garden shed, and they're not even done building it. Capturing something out of Westminster Cathedral is a fantasy. You might as well go questing after the Unholy Grail or the Gem of Amara while you're at it!"

"I can get it."

"And if you can't? You always make these grand overtures, but you have no idea if you'll be able to follow through! You don't plan! You don't care! You set us up—set *Drusilla* up—for one broken promise after another! When I told you to give her something to look forward to, I didn't mean an eternity of perpetual regret."

Spike opened his mouth to speak and then closed it again. He cocked his head to one side and watched the tightness of Darla's features soften ever so slightly before he spoke. "I'm not him," he said at last.

Across from him, Darla's jaw clenched and her eyes fell.

"I may be seven shades of awful," he continued, "but I think you know that *disloyal* doesn't make the list. Never been a piker in matters of the heart. If I make Dru a promise, it's because I intend to keep it."

Darla didn't raise her eyes. "Angelus was loyal, too—until he wasn't."

Spike put a hand on her shoulder. "First of all, he was an arse long before he left us."

Darla shot Spike a glare and batted his hand away.

"Hey, you never could spell *Angelus* without *anus*." Spike shrugged. "Second of all, this job is gonna be as easy as the wind blows. It's all there in that old newspaper. They're pushing to finish that great eyesore of a building, and apparently the construction poses a risk to some of the artifacts already housed inside it, so they're moving a load of fancy baubles across town to the Church of the Most Precious Blood. I know what you're thinking—great name for a pub, a bit wasted on a church, but there it is. And guess which relic is gonna be in the mix, guarded by nothing more than a handful of pissant priests?"

Darla narrowed her eyes, but Spike could tell she was softening to the idea. "And while we're at it, we can snatch whatever other trinkets they've got on hand to secure ourselves a bit of spending money. See? That's me, looking ahead. It's gonna be a snap. Well—probably a few snaps. Dru likes it when their necks go all the way backward."

Darla shook her head. "What if you disappoint her?"

"But what if I *don't*?"

"I'm ready," said Drusilla. She emerged through the opening in the wall, straightening the cuffs on her coat as she stepped out. "Do you think those funny guild people will ask us to sign their big leather book in blood again?"

"I told you last time, dear," said Darla, giving Spike one last warning glance before she turned to Drusilla, "nobody asked you to sign it with blood. In fact, it made a few people very uncomfortable that you did. There was a full inkwell right there on the table for you to use."

"What's wrong with signing in blood?" said Drusilla. "Signatures always feel fancier when you make them in blood."

"I think their main objection was that you didn't use your own," said Darla. "It's rather discourteous to bleed someone else's familiar. So few vampires even keep them anymore."

"They were just being selfish," said Spike. He reached inside the hovel and scooped his own coat off the ground. "Well? Let's get this over with. I wager ten shillings Count Orlok tries to flirt with you again, Darla."

"You don't have ten shillings."

"I will after the wilting cabbage makes his move."

CHAPTER SIX

The London Vampires' Guild had been housed in the same imposing Romanesque crypt in Highgate since the cemetery was established—and the guild itself had been around long before then. Prior to Highgate, their meetings had been conducted in a derelict old mansion, on the floor of an abandoned tannery, and, on at least one notable occasion, aboard a sloop moored on the Thames. The latter had resulted in four guild members' deaths and a formal grievance from the Dock Goblins' Union—and thus all subsequent assemblies had been held on solid ground. The stately old crypt suited the guild.

"See, this is the sort of thing I'm talking about," Darla mused as they approached. "I would just kill for a nice mausoleum to call home. Something elegant with lots of marble."

Spike gave a noncommittal nod. "The columns are okay. Bit old-fashioned for my taste. I like a place with a bit more character. Do you remember that massive château in Bordeaux?"

Darla nodded. "Angelus got the doorman to invite us all inside," she recalled, "and then you killed that maid with the funny laugh."

"I remember," said Drusilla. "I liked her. She tasted like merlot."

"That's the one," Spike said. "I could live in a fancy château like that. Good, thick curtains for the daytime. Nice view after the sun goes down. What about you, Dru?"

Drusilla considered. "Do you know that feeling you get," she asked, "when you're killing somebody, and they haven't quite given up? That fleeting moment when *you* know they're already dead, but *they* still haven't figured it out yet?"

"We were talking about where we'd like to live," said Spike.

"Yes," said Drusilla. "That's where."

"That's my girl," said Darla, patting Drusilla's cheek. She mounted the marble steps and rapped on the wide door of the crypt.

One gaunt steward and a spiral stairway later, the three of them had descended into the guild hall. Their shoes clicked loudly against the floor as they walked, echoing through an orchard of thick stone columns that blossomed into sweeping arches and formed a vaulted ceiling. Torchlight flickered from sconces along the far wall, making the shadows between each column ripple like water. The four high-backed seats of the chancellors sat empty against the far wall.

To the left of these was a tall, broad-shouldered figure, his back to the visiting trio and his attention fixed on a potted plant. The plant had wide, waxy leaves and was seated like a prized possession on a plinth in front of an ornamental alcove. Matching pots stood on matching plinths all along the wall. "Ah, Darla," purred a voice as deep as the patches of darkness into which it bounced and echoed. "Do come in."

The man took his time pouring a gentle trickle over the plant from a slim watering can. When he was satisfied, he finally straightened and turned to face his guests. He wore a finely tailored suit that was at least half a century out of fashion, and his accent was faintly Eastern European, although its syllables had been shaped by the passage of time to something more or less British. "It has been too long."

"Much," Darla agreed, stepping forward to greet him. "Lord Ruthven, you remember Drusilla." She gestured behind her. "And Spike."

Lord Ruthven's expression remained impeccably serene, although it was the sort of manufactured serenity that might strain a muscle in Lord Ruthven's temple if he remained so serene for too long. "Indeed," he managed. "All too well."

Spike put far less effort into an unenthusiastic smile and a casual wave.

"I take it you intend to remain in London for the long term?" said Ruthven, turning his attention away again and striding casually to the next potted plant. "Splendid. Splendid. I was hoping you were not simply passing through. We shall have to update the registry. Where are you currently lodging?"

"Our current residence is . . . less than ideal," Darla said. "We were actually hoping the guild might be of some assistance on that front."

"I see," said Ruthven, his eyes flicking up from his watering. "I would be happy to have Polidori put you on the list for re-homing— but, to be quite honest, habitation requests are very low on the guild's priority list right now. London's vampire community has more pressing concerns that demand our attention at present."

"Now that you bring it up, what exactly *do* London's vampires need you for?" said Spike. Darla shot him an acid glare. "Just out of curiosity," Spike added.

"I swear—" Darla began.

"It is fine." Lord Ruthven shook his head, regarding Spike pityingly. "This one is but an infant. He does not remember the years before our venerable society was formed."

"Did the vampires back then eat people without changing into their dinner jackets first?" Spike rolled his eyes.

"Mm." Ruthven regarded Spike with all the patience of a first-year teacher watching a student eat paste. "There was a time," he said, "prior to our formation, when vampires made themselves infamous for lurid acts and wanton violence. There were roving street gangs. The Damned Crew, the Scourers, the Hawkubites."

"Ugh. I knew a Hawkubite," said Darla. "He threw up half a flower girl on my favorite shoes once. Never even apologized."

Ruthven nodded grimly before continuing: "These overt displays of depravity drew increased public scrutiny. With increased scrutiny came the inevitable daylight raids, holy-water showers, and wooden stakes. It was not a pleasant period for our community. So, in the interest of preserving the grand traditions of the London undead, the Vampiric Convention of 1714 agreed that an association of respectable vampires would decide on and enforce certain standards of sinister behavior to be observed within the limits of the city. Any vampires unable to control themselves would be exiled. Or worse."

"Where do you send them?" Drusilla asked. "The ones who can't control themselves?"

"To *less civilized* environs," answered Ruthven heavily. "Like Bristol. Or Manchester."

"Hey. I like Manchester," said Spike.

"This does not surprise me," said Ruthven flatly. He set the slim watering can on the plinth beside him. "I don't suppose you know much about horticulture? It can be a rewarding discipline. Take this specimen." He gestured at his plant. It had broad green leaves that hung over the side of the pot. "*Aspidistra elatior.* A hardy breed. It develops slowly but is difficult to kill. It also loathes the sun—all traits with which I can empathize." He brushed one of the fronds delicately. "Direct sunlight would scorch the poor thing's leaves, yet we all seem to crave that which could ruin us, don't we?" He gave Spike a knowing look.

"Your plants like to live dangerously?"

"In a manner of speaking." Ruthven allowed himself a weak smile. "My perennial pets require at least a modicum of indirect sunlight, much to my chagrin. Fortunately, our hall is equipped to provide such ambient illumination."

He pulled a cord on the wall, and from high above there came a faint grating noise, and then the recess behind the plant was bathed in a column of moonlight. "The architects were very careful about the angles on these skylights," Ruthven went on. "In the heat of day, they allow the sun's rays to pierce only into the alcoves and no further."

In the soft glow of the moonbeams, Spike could see iron chains and what appeared to be wrist restraints bolted to the walls of the recess. "I'm guessing that particular renovation wasn't installed with a houseplant in mind," he noted.

"No, indeed," Ruthven confirmed darkly. "There are, from time to time, those vampires who indulge too freely in cravings that could ruin us all. I'm sure you can imagine. Not every offense earns one a simple trip to Manchester. Ashes, as it happens, make for superb soil additives. Plants love them. Did you know?"

Spike shook his head. "Just here to sign the book, mate."

"Of course." Ruthven nodded. "Polidori," he called over his shoulder, "fetch the register, please."

A short, sickly-looking man stepped forward from behind the dais and bowed. His eyes darted to Drusilla, and then he scurried away, the click of shoes echoing through the chamber as he hurried off into the shadows.

"Are you the only sitting chancellor tonight?" Darla asked before the silence could become awkward.

Ruthven's brow arched. "Until the next convention, I am the *only* chancellor," he said. "Claudia and Varney are dead. Count Orlok has been missing for several months. We still have about a dozen enforcers and runners, but they are all growing nervous."

"Has it really got so bad?" said Darla.

Ruthven shook his head solemnly. "The demonic clans have been centralizing under a new leader, a Hastam demon called Gunnar. They've been growing increasingly brazen, and tensions have risen. Humans are beginning to take notice. A few of ours got mixed in with a very public mess right on palace grounds a few months ago, and Prince Edward mobilized Blackhearth."

Darla drew a breath through her teeth. "Buckingham's secret guards?"

"The operatives rounded up the guilty culprits, as well as half a dozen additional vampires for good measure. Their teams struck during the day while we were most powerless to defend ourselves. I suspect it was Edward's not-so-subtle way of making a point. As always, the paranormal details were kept hush-hush from the humans. The royals don't want panic in the streets—especially since so many of the blue bloods are something more than human themselves—but the message to the monster masses was clear enough."

They were quiet for a moment.

It was Drusilla who broke the silence. "Royal blood isn't really blue," she said. "I know. I checked."

Ruthven narrowed his eyes at her. "*That* is precisely the sort of behavior that you will *not* engage in while you are in London. We do not need anyone poking the proverbial hornets' nest."

"Can't get the honey without poking the nest," countered Drusilla.

"Hornets do not produce honey," said Ruthven, picking up his watering can again. "They produce *pain*."

"Mm." Drusilla smiled.

"We get it," said Spike. "The locals are jumpy, so keep our noses clean, and no hunting on palace grounds. Understood."

"I don't think you do understand," said Ruthven. He turned and proceeded toward a third plinth. "If you intend to remain in London, you must accept that *all* hunting is to be strictly limited. Attacks against nobles and the gentry are entirely prohibited any-where in the city, and even the dregs should be eaten sparingly, if at all."

He began to calmly water the plant in front of him and then paused, eying one dull brown leaf amid the green ones.

Spike stared at him. "No killing gentry? Seriously? What if—hypothetically—they were very rude and had terrible taste in literature, and you were fairly certain nobody would miss them much?"

"Hypothetically?" Lord Ruthven raised an eyebrow, his gaze darting to Spike and back to the plant in front of him. With a quick flick of his wrist, he snipped off the wilted leaf at the stem with his fingernails and let the offending frond flutter to the granite floor. "No exceptions. It's not worth the risk."

"A vampire has to eat!"

"There are other cities," said Ruthven. "Other countries, even. Consider an evening trip to France when you wish to feast."

"France?" Spike sneered.

"You were literally fantasizing about moving to Bordeaux not twenty minutes ago," Darla reminded him.

"That's different," said Spike, straightening his lapels with a tug. "Nobody was trying to push us out of our home back then."

"Nobody is being pushed out," Ruthven said. "But when you are in London, you are a civilized vampire. You do not act like some masked highwayman on a remote forest path. It is in the best interests of our kind for the citizens of this city to believe that the worst thing awaiting them outside their front doors is the traffic on Fleet Street."

Spike opened his mouth, and then he closed it again. His eyes glinted in the torchlight.

"Ah!" Ruthven glanced up as the short, bustling servant returned with the heavy leather book in his arms. "Thank you, Polidori. That will be all." Ruthven dismissed the man, who vanished eagerly back into the shadows.

"Up you go," said Darla. She and Drusilla stepped onto the dais.

Before Spike could join, Lord Ruthven slid into his path. "The guild was proud to hear that the last slayer fell to London fangs," he said.

"You're welcome?" said Spike.

"However," Ruthven continued, "the London you have returned

to is not the London that you left. You have much to learn about discretion, and in times such as these, we do not have the luxury of extending the sort of allowances we once did."

"You think I can't control myself?" Spike's jaw tightened.

Ruthven was unflappable. He tilted his head, watching as Spike clenched his fists. "Can you?"

Spike bit his tongue. On the dais, Drusilla was already bent over the ancient book, adding her name in blood.

"Hmm." Ruthven nodded. "Remember: The book is a contract. Signing your name is a solemn oath to respect the decisions of our guild while you reside within the limits of the city. Can you make such a commitment?"

"I keep my promises," Spike growled.

"Good." Ruthven stepped aside to let him pass. "I do not wish to dampen such a flame as yours, young one." His voice remained exquisitely calm, but his eyes bored into Spike as he spoke. Under his foot, the solitary brown leaf crunched faintly. "Nor would I take any pleasure in *extinguishing* it."

Spike met his gaze without comment before brushing past him to scrawl his signature under Drusilla's, dotting the *i* so emphatically, he pierced the page.

When the jittery Polidori had, at last, been instructed to escort the trio outside, Darla held back. "You two go ahead," she said. "I'd like to have a private word with Lord Ruthven first."

Spike arched an eyebrow but shrugged and escorted Drusilla up the stairwell.

"Something troubles you," said Ruthven. "Your wayward Angelus?"

Darla shook her head. "It's not the one who abandoned me that I'm concerned about—but rather the ones who remain by my side." She hesitated. "Drusilla is terrible and powerful in her own special ways, but she takes so much looking after. I fear Spike is not yet equal to the task. He has potential, but much to learn."

"As did we all, once," Ruthven said charitably. He gave the cord along the wall another tug, and the alcoves fell into darkness once again. "I seem to recall more than a few instances when even you needed to be pulled out of the fire."

"Precisely my point," said Darla. "I had the Order of Aurelius to look out for me when I was Drusilla's age—and you and the other chancellors when I was older. I need to know that the guild will watch over her as it has watched over me."

Ruthven's brow creased. "You are held in the highest regard in these halls, my dear Darla. So long as your kin travel with you, they travel under the full protection of the guild. You know that. Our doors are always open to you."

Darla's mouth tightened. "Yes. But what if my kin were to reside in London *without* me? Could I be sure that Drusilla would enjoy the same resources and hospitality?"

Ruthven gave Darla an appraising look. "I see. You plan to leave them." He pursed his lips. "It is only because they are your family that the guild has overlooked their many transgressions in the past," he answered bluntly. "*You* have earned special consideration, Darla. Your kin have not."

"I would be in your debt."

"And in the past, a debt might have sufficed. But these are trying times."

"What could I offer you to ensure that they *did* fall under the guild's full protection?"

Ruthven considered. "Blackhearth," he said at last.

Darla's brow furrowed. "Buckingham's best?"

"They know our ways, move on our kind during the daylight, and wield holy weapons against which we cannot defend. If we kill ten of them, they return with fifty. Even I do not know how many they number. They have been relentless in their persecution of our community. We are on the verge of canceling Darkmarket this year."

"You're not going to cancel Darkmarket. Vampires come from thousands of miles for Darkmarket."

"And it would be a mark of unspeakable shame on our organization to admit that we cannot host it," Ruthven agreed. "And yet it would not be half as calamitous as allowing our brethren to be corralled together in one place, ripe to be slaughtered by the humans in a daytime purge worthy of the history books."

"It's that bad?"

Ruthven nodded solemnly. "You once had connections with a few members of the aristocracy, as I recall. Perhaps you might call in a personal favor or two on behalf of the guild? Even a temporary détente would suffice, and—of course, we are eager to see the release of Count Orlok back into the night, if he still lives."

"I manage to convince the royals to call off their guard dogs and let Orlok go, and you'll guarantee Drusilla guild benefits befitting a senior vampire?"

Ruthven gave a nod. "I believe that would be a worthy exchange—if it can be done. Do you still have the ear of one of the royal family?"

"No." Darla squared her jaw. "But I know someone who does."

A few minutes later, Darla emerged from the crypt, stepping back out into the crisp night air. Spike and Drusilla were leaning on headstones, waiting.

"Have a nice chat?" asked Spike. "Don't suppose you're gonna tell us what that was all about?"

"Private matter," said Darla.

"I can't believe the nerve of that pompous git," Spike grumbled.

"You're lucky that *pompous git* didn't have you exiled for insolence," Darla said. "You do know that pretending to be likable once in a while is a real and viable option, right?"

"I am likable," said Spike. "I'm very likable."

"I like you," confirmed Drusilla.

"See?"

"A glowing endorsement," said Darla. "Although you've liked a lot of questionable things, Drusilla. Before we let you keep Spike, you liked that doll you made for yourself out of the leftover pieces of a cat. We threw that thing out eventually."

"I miss Mister Sticky Whiskers," said Drusilla fondly. "Do you think Angelus will bring me a new one when he comes home?"

Spike cringed. "Lord Ruthven likes me, too," he said hastily. "He likes me so much he gave me that tremendous tip about how to procure that rascally relic for Dru."

"He did no such thing." Darla stopped in her tracks. "Spike. Tell me you're not still thinking about pulling off a ridiculous daylight heist. You wouldn't. Not now. Were you even listening back there?"

"Absolutely! I'm always listening. Increased pressure on the vampire community. Fear of the paranormal on the rise. Blah-blah. That's why a daylight robbery is such a brilliant idea."

"You are officially off your trolley."

"Think about it! Obviously, appearing in broad daylight is the *last* thing any sane vampire would ever be suspected of trying. Right?"

"Right," said Darla slowly, like she was talking to a dullard. "Because it's utterly mad."

"Exactly!" Spike nodded. "So, if we do it, vampires would be the last monsters that those meddling monarchists from Buckingham would ever suspect were behind it!"

Darla closed her eyes. "And what if you bungle the whole thing?"

"Fair point, yes. But counterpoint—what if I *don't*?" Spike grinned broadly. "What if we actually pull it off? Daylight robbery, committed by vampires—can you even imagine? It would be the stuff of legends! Eat your heart out, Count Dracula. You don't see that bloated blowhard braving the daylight. They would write stories about us instead."

Darla opened her eyes again and fixed Spike with a cold stare and a raised eyebrow. "What makes you so confident that you can even get your hands on that infernal finger?"

"Not *me*, my dear Darla. I am confident that *we* can get our hands on that infernal finger."

"We? Oh, *I'm* a part of this, too?"

"Unless you'd like to abandon us? That's fine. We're getting used to being abandoned. We can pull the job without you. Dru will get over it eventually, I'm sure. Isn't that right, Dru?"

"You don't want to be with us, Grandmother?" said Drusilla. Her eyes were suddenly glistening in the moonlight. "I thought you liked being with us."

Darla pursed her lips and crossed her arms over her chest. "That is *not* fair."

"Nope!" Spike smiled. "But it *is* effective. So, you're in?"

Darla looked far from convinced. "Care to enlighten me as to how three vagrant vampires are supposed to hold up a moving carriage in the middle of London in broad daylight?"

"Well, like Ruthven said, we don't act like masked highwaymen on some remote path," he said. "We act like masked highwaymen in a city where the worst thing people can imagine is traffic."

"I already hate this."

Spike shot her a wink. "Do you remember the mountain troll who kept following us when we cut through that farmland outside Munich?"

Darla narrowed her eyes at the sudden change of topic. "That thing was almost as dense as you are. I had to throw something at his head to get him to sod off."

Drusilla smiled at the memory. "It was a goat. You threw a goat at him."

"That's right," said Spike.

"And?" pressed Darla.

Spike grinned. "How's your throwing arm?"

CHAPTER SEVEN

Spike and Drusilla moved silently into position beneath an oblivious city. Well, they moved somewhat silently. In truth, there was a considerable amount of whinging and cursing as their bulky cloaks got snagged on pipe fittings or dragged through puddles in the dark.

Spike felt more than a little ridiculous in his new getup. *Plague doctor raiment* had sounded so stylishly macabre when he had picked them up, but now he and Dru were both wearing what amounted to thick leather dresses with belts around their midsections and floppy black hats. The cloaks were ancient, they were heavy, and they were much too long—had the previous owners been *giants*? But Spike knew he would be grateful for their bulky fabric once they breached the sunlight. It had been a stroke of luck that the Shady Shop had the outfits in stock at all, and all the more that Gus had been willing to give them to Spike on credit— vintage plague masks included. The masks did not actually smell like death. They smelled like Earl Grey. Spike wasn't sure why, but he had felt mildly cheated by that detail.

"This is it," Spike said, squinting at the markings on the grate above them. "Stamford Street and Blackfriars Road are right above us, so now we just need to listen for Darla's signal. Time to put on the manky masks."

"I like my mask," Drusilla said, holding her hat in one hand so that she could slide the mask over her head with the other. It was a crude, simple design: a long leather beak bordered by two circular glass lenses in the eyeholes. The whole thing was affixed to a sort of stiff hood that draped over the cloak for maximum coverage. Once she had it in place, she plopped her hat back over the top of it, tilting her head left and right experimentally. "It makes me feel like a big black bird," she said, her voice muffled from within the mask.

"Well, I don't like mine," grunted Spike. "It's too tight, and it smells like stale tea. I do, however, like not dying in flames, so here we go."

"You look like a bird, too." Drusilla giggled as Spike fidgeted. "Like a crow with a funny hat on."

"Well, I guess that makes us a proper *murder*, doesn't it?" His voice echoed uncomfortably from within the thing, and he had no peripheral vision at all. But it would have to do.

By now, the coach carrying the Relic of Saint Agabus would be crossing Westminster Bridge into Waterloo. In a few minutes, it would be directly above them. The plan was simple—Spike liked simple. Darla would cause a distraction to halt traffic, and then he and Drusilla would pop out, grab the relic, and slip back into the sewers. In and out in under five minutes, and then all three of them would meet back at the basement to look over their haul.

Even Lord Ruthven couldn't complain. Any priest they might need to murder in the process would be neither a noble nor a merchant, and the real killer would be the traffic.

"What do you think Darla's signal is going to sound like?" asked Drusilla. She swung her arms within her floppy sleeves as she waited. "I was thinking it would probably sound like a whole big swarm of angry butterflies."

"Butterflies don't make noise, love."

"A whole big swarm."

"We'll know the signal when we hear it," said Spike.

From above them came the steady *clop-clop* of hoofbeats and the rattle of wheels on cobblestones. A bell rang in the distance.

Spike's nose began to itch. He nudged his mask around in an effort to rub the spot against the inside of the leather, but to no avail. The leather was too tight for him to squeeze a hand up under the mask's bottom skirt, but he tried anyway.

Above them, the street suddenly erupted with noise. First came a distant muffled shout, and then the thunderous crash and the splintering of wood as something very heavy smashed into the cobblestones not half a block away. Horses neighed and voices shouted—the whole block flooded with a cacophony of urgent sounds—but the steady rhythm of carriage wheels had ground to a halt.

Spike yanked his hand clumsily out of the mask and jumped onto the ladder. "That's our cue!" They had to strike now or miss the fleeting window of opportunity. He gave the grate above him a shove. It didn't budge. He adjusted his position and drove a shoulder into it. It wobbled slightly upward, but he could feel a heavy weight slam it shut again. He cursed and gritted his teeth. "Someone's parked on top of the bloody grate!"

"The relic," said Drusilla, staring through filmy glass lenses at the ceiling. "It's right above us. I can feel it."

Spike slid back down the ladder and tilted his mask this way and that as he got his bearings in the gloom. Visibility through the infernal eyeholes was awful. "Come on!" He grabbed Drusilla's hand. "There's another ladder at the far end of the block. We'll need to leg it."

To the casual observer standing near the corner of Stamford and Blackfriars, the violent ejection of a rolltop desk from the fourth-story window of a nearby building might have been startling enough even without the mayhem that followed it. The desk certainly startled the carriage horses, in front of whom it exploded as it hit the ground, spraying splinters and loose paper. For the record, Darla would have preferred to launch something classier, like a piano—but sadly, the tenant in apartment forty-two had not been musically inclined. The rolltop served its purpose, though. Travel in both directions lurched to a stop as horses reared up and carriages tipped precariously.

Darla was already gone by the time the last remains of the desk had clattered to a stop. The only reason she had involved herself in the caper to begin with was the tenuous hope that one last grand adventure might finally quell the restless discontent that had hung over their family since Beijing.

Had she stayed to watch the aftermath of her contribution, she might have borne witness to the sewer grate on the opposite end of the block flipping into the air a few moments later and two figures—not unlike fourteenth-century plague doctors—vaulting from the depths into the sunlight. It is, perhaps, for the best that she did not remain in her position to see what happened next.

Spike's vision went white as he hopped out of the sewer and into the light of day. He squinted into the glare. Ahead of him, pale images began to emerge—brick buildings, carriages, and so many people walking, milling about, gawking. He cursed under his breath as he willed his eyes to fully adjust.

Daylight.

He could feel the sun's rays pressing against his cloak like the needle-sharp points of a million invisible swords. He should not be here. Drusilla should not be here. Vampires were not made for the daytime.

"Which one?" Drusilla's muffled voice came from beside him.

Spike scanned the carts and carriages around them. Hansom cab . . . dairy cart . . . no, no, no. He strained his eyes. Halfway up the block there was a sturdy-looking coach trimmed with elegant silver metalwork. He pointed a black-gloved finger at the vehicle. "That'll be the one."

They both raced toward the coach, but Drusilla got there first. Even in her heavy robes, she moved with grace and power as she vaulted to the driver's box.

"Wh-what are you?" stammered the driver.

Spike could hear the smile in Drusilla's voice when she answered. "We're a *murder.*"

Spike grinned. He loved watching Drusilla work. She was out of place up here in the light of day, surrounded by so many dull humans—she was a wildfire in a city of fluttering candles. Of course, she would actually *be* a fire if they didn't finish the job quickly and return underground. He shook his head and brought his focus back to the task at hand.

Spike grabbed the door to the coach and ripped it clear off its hinges while Drusilla dealt with the driver. He peered inside. A woman in a floral dress let out a shriek and pressed herself as far as she could into the corner of the bench.

Spike swiveled his head to peer through the foggy lenses at the compartment. A thick wicker suitcase and an expensive purse occupied the seat across from the woman, but otherwise the coach was empty. He turned his eyes back to the woman. "You," he said accusingly, "don't look like a priest."

The woman squeaked incomprehensibly.

"Sodding hell," said Spike.

Drusilla's feet landed on the cobblestones beside him as Spike spun out of the cab. In his haste, his baggy sleeve caught the shredded metal of what was left of the hinge. There was a feeble ripping sound, and in an instant, searing pain blossomed through his arm. He slapped a gloved hand over the hole, but a wisp of smoke already hung in the air. He grunted.

"Are you all right?" Drusilla tilted her head, birdlike.

"Wrong coach," he growled, his eyes already scanning for the correct one.

Ahead, carriages were beginning to navigate their horses carefully around the pile that had once been a writing desk. Somebody on the sidewalk was yelling something and pointing in their direction. Spike could feel eyes on them. The vague possibility that his brilliant plan might go wrong—which had seemed like such a distant and trifling threat an hour ago—was now barreling toward him faster than a rolltop. This was precisely why he hated making plans. It was so much easier to deal with things going wrong when you didn't have a lot of false hope that they were supposed to go right.

Drusilla put a hand to her temple. "I can feel it, Spike. The relic. I think it's moving away."

Crossing the intersection was a simple brown coach. As it turned to navigate the debris, Spike could see the driver was dressed in a humble Catholic cassock.

With a snarl, he took off running once more. Keeping one hand clapped over his torn sleeve was going to make breaking necks a little trickier, but he had killed people under worse circumstances. He could still do this. His whole body felt as if it were beginning to boil inside the heavy robes. If he had been properly alive, he would have been sweating buckets—he might as well have been wearing a diving suit to swim through lava. He dodged past startled pedestrians and vaulted over a battered file drawer, cocking his mask to the right for an instant to confirm Drusilla was still at his side. She was.

And then Spike found himself smiling in spite of it all. For all that was going wrong, something about this caper still felt right. The coach was twenty feet ahead, and they were gaining on it. Fifteen. Ten.

And then in an instant—before either of them could catch hold of the bustling cart—the air ahead became thick and heavy with swirling, foggy wisps. They slowed as the world around them grew more and more opaque, as if they had been swimming in a clear stream and something below had churned up the river bottom.

Spike tried to wipe off the lenses on his mask to no effect. The

oily smoke swelled and thickened until soon the coach was completely enveloped and obscured by the dark cloud. From within the
roiling gray mass, horses brayed and then fell silent.

"What . . . the . . . hell?" Spike panted. He and Drusilla slowed
to a halt in the middle of the street. He could only just make out
the faces of confused passersby through the haze. Whatever this
mess was, it was concentrated on the coach.

All around them, people were yelling and pointing. And then,
from out of the crowd, a man in an immaculate gray suit with a
bloodred necktie emerged. He wore dark-tinted glasses with circular frames that made his ashen face look like a skull. The black
hair pushed back on his head failed to fully conceal a pair of obsidian horns. He approached the cloud.

"Demon," Spike grumbled. "Hey, mate! That's our mark! Go
find your own!"

A second, third, and fourth demon materialized around the
clouded coach. They were dressed to match the first, and all three
carried charcoal-gray satchels. As one, they slid inside the cloud.

"If those scaly bastards think they can—" Spike let the thought
hang in the air.

A moment later, the figures reemerged, their packs noticeably
heavier. As quickly as they had appeared, they vanished back into
the crowd, and the darkness began to dissipate. It bled outward,
filling the whole street with fading oily smoke.

Through the haze, Spike could see that the doors to the coach
were hanging open. He jogged closer and poked his head inside.
The bodies of two priests were slumped over in the cabin, a wooden
chest open and empty between them. A handful of psalmbooks
and loose papers lay on the floor, soaking up blood. No relics.

Spike cursed. A heavy shoulder slammed against his the moment he dropped back to the cobblestone, and he turned to find himself face-to-face with the demon in the tinted glasses. The figure wrinkled his nose and peered down at Spike over the top of the frames. His eyes were blacker than the lenses.

"Thought I smelled a couple of blood rats." He sneered. His voice was a sibilant buzz, like something between the drone of a hornet and the hiss of a snake.

Spike seethed. "That was *our* coach you just robbed."

"Was it?" The demon straightened and adjusted his tie. "I was under the impression it belonged to the church." He was at least half a foot taller than Spike. Spike's plague robes would have probably fit him perfectly. Bastard.

"It was *our* robbery," Spike pressed, "that you just robbed us of . . . robbing." He gritted his teeth.

"I see." The demon looked from Spike to Drusilla and back. "In that case, you're welcome."

"Welcome? For what?" Spike snarled.

"My employer sent us out on a very simple mission," the demon answered evenly. "If your little stunt had been successful . . ." He nodded toward the remains of the desk behind them. "If you had snatched up something that Gunnar wanted—in his territory no less—then he would have had to deploy a very different team to execute a very different sort of mission. How lucky for you that you did not. You would do well, in the future, to stay out of our way."

Spike's eyes narrowed.

Drusilla put a hand on his arm and stepped between the two of them. "I think," she said, leaning in toward the ashen-faced demon, "it's a *badger*."

The demon raised an eyebrow. "A badger?"

Drusilla nodded. "The thing that's going to kill you. I think it's a badger."

The demon opened his mouth, then closed it again. Drusilla had that effect on people.

From somewhere up the street came a shrill blast from a police whistle. A voice from somewhere within the growing crowd called: "Sisseroth. Let's go!"

The demon shook his head and turned away from Spike and Drusilla. "Scurry back to your sewer, little rats."

The smoke was clearing, and the sidewalks around them were filling with more onlookers by the minute. In a blink, the demon had already vanished into the chaos. Where had he gone? Spike's arm was throbbing where the sunlight had found its way in through the rip in his robes, and his head was swimming from the heat. More police whistles pierced the general hubbub, and someone nearby let out a scream.

Spike sighed. Time to go.

In another minute, he and Drusilla were back beneath the streets of Waterloo. From above them, the sounds of muffled shouts grew fainter and fainter as they made their way gradually back toward the hideout. Spike ripped the mask off his face. That had been an unmitigated disaster.

"Well? Did you get anything good?" Darla greeted them at the basement door. Her face fell as she saw their expressions. "It was the desk, wasn't it? Not big enough? I knew I should have held out for a piano."

"It wasn't the desk," said Spike. "There were other complications." He winced as he ripped the cloak off himself. The scar on his arm was red and blistering. It looked like a map of the Philippines drawn by a disturbed cartographer.

"We got nothing," moaned Drusilla. "Not even the ickle finger."

"Nothing?"

"A pack of tossers snatched the loot before we got the chance," Spike added. "Not just any tossers, either. Demons. Organized demons. Demons with a boss. What's that name people keep saying? The big bad boss of the London underworld? Goober? Gunther?"

"Gunnar?" said Darla. "The head of the demon syndicate of London? The one Ruthven specifically warned you about not crossing?"

"Yeah. Gunnar. That sounds right. They were Gunnar's goons." Spike growled. "I should have taken that black-eyed bugger's head off."

"I should never have let you talk me into your stupid plan." Darla put a hand over her eyes. "You two managed to plow your way into a catastrophic failure—and a painfully public one at that—and your one regret is that you *missed* an opportunity to start an all-out war with a whole army of demons?"

"Angelus would have taken his head off," Drusilla said wistfully.

Spike glowered moodily.

Darla opened her mouth. Words seemed to be trying to form themselves in her throat, but ultimately, none of them dared the trip across her tongue. She turned from Drusilla to Spike, her eyes flashing between exasperation and disbelief. At length, she pursed her lips and went back inside without saying anything.

"Do you think she's cross with us?" said Drusilla.

"She was probably hoping we would bring her one of those big hats that bishops wear," said Spike. "She'll get over it."

Drusilla sighed. "I only wanted one teensy relic."

Spike bit his lip, watching Dru's shoulders sag. They had been so close. That pesky pinkie had practically been in their grasp. Just being close to it, Drusilla had seemed more herself, more excited to be on the hunt, less anchored to the past.

"I'll get it back for you." Spike flexed his sore arm experimentally. "Soon as the sun's gone down, love. I promise."

"Do you even know where they've taken it?" she asked, dispirited.

"Sure," he said. "The hornets' nest."

CHAPTER EIGHT

Spike's arm was still aching as he crossed the lamp-lit streets that evening. He was alone, which suited his mood fine. Darla had gone out to clear her head the moment the sun was down, and Drusilla's melancholy had only gotten worse. She had committed herself to an endless series of compulsive if dispirited tarot readings, the results of which she was not inclined to share with anyone. If Spike hoped to improve her outlook toward a future with him—a future free of her sour-faced sire—then getting that pilfered pinkie back was essential.

He needed to find Gunnar. He was just going to have a friendly chat with the fellow. If everything went smoothly, Spike would be returning home in a few hours' time with a relic for Drusilla that was sure to wipe any thoughts of gallivanting across the globe after Angelus out of her mind. If everything went not-so-smoothly, well, at least not-so-smoothly would be familiar territory.

The tinkly bell on the door of the Shady Shop rang as Spike slipped inside.

"Welcome back!" Gus called happily from behind the counter. "You're gettin' to be one of my best customers. What'll it be today? Poisons? Restraints? We just got in a batch of adorable porcelain cats, if you're looking for knickknacks. The wee rascals are engaged in all manner of wickedness. Look—this one has just eaten a postman. She's all covered in hand-painted viscera. Very droll. Very collectible."

"Information," said Spike. "I'm looking for a demon called Gunnar."

Gus blinked. "Gunnar?" he said. "As in Gunnar the *Dread Lord of London Town*?"

"There is no way people are actually calling him *Dread Lord*."

"He just called himself that a little while back," Gus said, "and I guess not a lot of folks wanted to argue."

"I hate the dramatic ones," Spike groaned. "Right, well, where does a dread lord of London Town hang up his hat? Is there a demonic Buckingham? Evil Kensington?"

"Not that I'm aware of."

"What sort of self-respecting black-market peddler doesn't know where to find the biggest action in town?"

Gus shrugged. "I've got a map of haunted pubs, if you like."

"Hmph." Spike flexed his sore arm and turned back toward the door. "Thanks for nothing. See you around, Gus."

"You're sure you don't want to take another look at the cats? I got a cheeky calico here nibblin' on some brains. Cute as the dickens."

"Maybe next time."

Spike made his way back into the swirling London fog and down a few of the seedier backstreets, making inquiries along the way. Sadly, none of London's usual unusuals seemed able to help him.

He had just turned a corner when a flicker of movement caught his eye. Spike froze. A tingle wriggled up his spine, and with it, the pesky sensation that he was being watched.

"Oi!" he called. "If you're gonna spy on me, the least you could do is be a little more slick about it!"

There followed a resounding silence.

He hung a hard left and zigzagged up the next alley. His ears pricked at the sound of soft feet hurrying along the flagstones just ahead. He waited until the footfalls were almost upon him and then spun around the corner.

"Oh!" The woman in front of him had a simple dress, a neat bun in her hair, and a bright green pencil tucked behind one ear. As Spike materialized before her, she let out a startled squeak and nearly dropped an armful of papers. In her frantic efforts not to lose the whole stack, the top dozen or so sheets spun from her grip to the damp sidewalk.

"Excuse me," she said, kneeling to retrieve the fluttering pages.

Spike raised an eyebrow. "Miss Eriksson?"

She glanced up at him. "You!" she said. "Oh, how perfectly mortifying. To be honest, I wasn't entirely sure I didn't imagine you. I was not at my best last time. There are occasions when I am not an absolute disaster, I assure you."

Spike appraised the woman. As quick meals went, she did look considerably more palatable today. Her heartbeat rang through the night like a dinner bell. Page three had spun to a stop at his feet, and Spike bent and picked it up. "Your book?" he asked. His eyes scanned the page. "*Bathed in moonlight . . . a scream pierced the night.* You really are writing a pulpy monster story, aren't you?"

She plucked the page out of his hands and tucked it back onto the stack. "Nothing wrong with a few monsters," she said. "I happen to like monsters."

Spike grinned. "Do you, now?"

"Not going to say something biting?"

"When I decide to be *biting*, you'll know it. Trust me."

He picked page seven up from the gutter and shook a bit of mud from it. "What's it all about, then?" he asked. "Something fun? Modern London vampire? Debonair chap, good cheekbones, great hair?"

"Not exactly. It's set in a small village in Eastern Europe, about a hundred years ago."

"Ugh. Of course it is." Spike scanned the page in his hand. He squinted. "A hundred years ago? Shouldn't they be talking differently, then? Fancier? This dialogue just sounds like people."

She shook her head. "I hate stories that put on airs and try to sound old-fashioned. *Her visage was one of effulgent beauty*, and all that nonsense. If I wanted to read an old book, I'd read an old book. There are libraries full of old books."

Spike cleared his throat. "Nothing wrong with *effulgent*."

"Just say *glowing*. People know what *glowing* means." She shrugged and looked down at the page. "It may not always be exactly accurate, but the words *feel* right. And how a story makes you feel always seemed more important to me than some antiquated vocabulary lesson."

Spike had stopped paying attention. He could practically feel the warmth of the blood coursing through her veins. In the back of his mind, he was weighing the likelihood that the guild would find out if he just murdered her here and dumped her body in the Thames. She didn't look like the sort of person anybody would miss tremendously. Argh. This was why he hadn't wanted to visit the sodding guild. They complicated everything and made an act as simple and wholesome as a casual evening murder out to be some terrible crime.

Spike picked the final page off the curb and handed it to her. "You always take your monster manuscripts for walks down shady streets in the middle of the night?" he asked.

"When and where I take my manuscripts for walks is nobody's business but my own," she answered. "For your information, some of us have responsibilities that occupy our daylight hours. I happen to have a prestigious position with the *Westminster Gazette*, thank you very much."

"Fetching biscuits and tea?"

She bristled. "Oh, never mind. It's a start. And I *am* going to be a real writer someday. Not that it's any of your business, but I'm out here tonight because there's a man who lives up the way who agreed to give me some editorial advice for a small fee. He's a very important man who works for Archibald Constable and Company. They were the ones who published Bram Stoker's latest horror."

"No. Tell me you're not a fan," said Spike.

"It's an absolute masterwork of the macabre. Have you read it?"

"I'm familiar," Spike growled. "Look, I've been doing so well *not* murdering you horribly, so if you don't mind, let's skip the bit where we talk about the sodding count."

"If you insist," she said, straightening the papers in her grip. "I do enjoy not being murdered."

"Apparently I'm not supposed to murder *anyone*." Spike sighed. "Especially not nobility. Firm rule about that. You're not nobility, are you?"

"Do I look like nobility?"

Spike shook his head. "Dregs?" he asked, brightening.

"Somewhere in between, I'd like to think," she said, a bit huffily.

"Mm." Spike considered. "The middle class is a bit of a gray area, to be honest. But you're probably all right. For now."

"That's a great comfort," she said. "Well? What about you? Why are *you* out in the middle of the night, haunting back alleys and startling unsuspecting women?"

"As it happens, I'm also on my way to meet someone important," said Spike. "Gonna practice a bit of diplomacy on the nobby gentry."

"You don't sound especially excited about it."

Spike shrugged. "Lately I've got a lot more comfortable around a bloody lip than a stiff upper one." He scowled. "I don't know why I'm telling *you* all this."

"Oh, come on. Talk. Everybody needs to unload feelings once in a while, even tough guys like you. Besides, what's the worst thing that could happen? Afraid I might put you in a story that nobody wants to publish?"

He huffed. "Maybe you should. A story about *me* would be loads better than *Frankenstein* or sodding *Dracula*."

Spike thought for a moment. This was stupid. He didn't need to *talk* about feelings. He occasionally needed to *kill people* about feelings, but that was different. On the other hand, he did have a lot going on in his head lately—what with keeping Drusilla from leaving him, keeping the guild from exiling him, and keeping Darla from tearing his head off. It couldn't hurt to release the pressure. Plus, he could always talk about feelings and *then* kill her, if the mood struck.

"It's just," he said, "things have got so much . . . *bigger*. It all used to be so simple. I used to like rolling up my sleeves and getting my hands dirty. But I became sort of a big deal. And now I keep needing to get bigger, just to hang on to it."

"If it's not making you happy, why bother?" said Miss Eriksson. "Who needs to be a big deal?"

Spike swallowed and scratched the back of his neck. "People don't leave you if you're a big deal," he said. "Besides, got to keep moving forward. I had to turn down a job offer just the other day. Almost wish I could have taken it. Used to love that line of work—and I could use the scratch—but it would've been a big step backward."

"Really?" she said. "You're saying you're above it now?"

"Yeah, so?" said Spike. "Maybe I am."

"Oh, excuse me! With all your whinging about nobby gentry and the like, I didn't realize I was talking to a fine lord."

"Lords have got nothing on me," Spike countered with a wry smile.

"Royalty, then?" Miss Eriksson teased, affecting a posh accent and puffing herself up. "No? Still too lowly? Am I in the presence of a venerable *god*?"

"Now you're getting it," Spike said, chuckling. "But not one of those ugly ones with a thousand tentacles and a sphincter for a face. One of the sexy ones. A god with style."

Miss Eriksson shook her head, smiling. "My mother used to tell me stories about the gods," she said. "Have you ever heard of Odin?"

"He's the one who looks like a pirate, right?" He put a hand over one eye.

"A little respect, if you please. Odin was the All-Father. God of the slain."

"As in the undead?" said Spike. "I'm liking him so far."

"He had temples and great halls dedicated to him, but he didn't like to sit idly on his throne. He carried his own spear into battle, explored the Nine Realms, and personally led a great hunt through the bitter winds of the winter sky every year. He never even caught the stag he was hunting. It always got away. It was always supposed to get away."

"Sounds like a pretty rubbish god," said Spike, "if he couldn't catch his prey."

She shrugged. "He was a god who knew what mattered."

"And what was that, then?"

"He knew that it wasn't about having a trophy mounted on your wall at the end of the day. It was about the hunt—about being in the world with your feet on the ground."

Spike considered this solemnly. "Sometimes the world beneath your feet changes so fast, there is no solid ground to stand on," he said with a sigh. "I'm on a hunt of my own, actually. Looking for a man—sort of. Not sure where he lives. You wouldn't happen to know the whereabouts of a chap called Gunnar? Might or might not also go by the embarrassingly showy title *Dread Lord of London Town*? No?"

"I met a Gustav once," she offered weakly. "Is Gunnar a friend?"

"Not exactly the word I'd use," said Spike. "Never met the bloke, myself, and the only people I know who have are either dead or wishing that he was."

"Why do you want to find him, then?"

"He's got something of mine, and I need it back."

"Why does this terrible person have something of yours?"

Spike clenched his fist. "For *reasons*."

"How come you don't ask your friends where to find him, then?"

Spike hesitated. "What friends?"

"The ones you said were wishing he was dead. If I had dealt with somebody as bad as all that and I wanted him dead, I'd probably work out where he lived pretty quickly."

Spike blinked. Hammond. Harry Hammond would definitely know where to find Gunnar.

"Huh," said Spike. "That's not a bad idea. Are people always this helpful when you don't murder them twice in a row? I might have to try it more often."

CHAPTER NINE

The Lang Building stood ahead of Spike, a run-down factory with a couple of boarded-up burned-out windows and a sagging roof. Tattered, fading signs depicting the remnants of a few smiling faces bespoke a time when the place had produced children's toys. The facility had long since been abandoned, and yet someone had taken the time to black out all the remaining windows.

Spike glanced up and down the empty street before slinking up to a delivery door. He rapped firmly on the chipped paint and waited.

In a few moments, a latch clicked and the door swung inward just enough to reveal the suspicious-looking face of a woman. She had deep brown skin and hair tied up at the back of her head that erupted in a dark halo of curls behind her.

"What do you want?" she said with all the hospitality of an ice pick.

"You should be careful about opening your door to strangers, love," said Spike. "Dangerous types out here at night."

The woman snorted, unimpressed. "Dangerous types in here at all hours." Her nose twitched and she appraised him, but then her shoulders relaxed and she let the door swing open wider. "By the smell of you, you couldn't cross this threshold without my invite even if you wanted to, though, could you?" She was wearing grubby coveralls, into the pocket of which she'd slipped something that looked a lot like a set of brass knuckles. A studded truncheon hung by her hip.

"Fair cop." Spike shrugged. He could tell that she wasn't a vampire, but she was clearly no stranger to the midnight monster scene. "You've got a good nose. Gonna invite me in?"

"I've also got a pulse and a brain. So probably not."

"Spike!" Hammond's voice boomed from behind the woman. She grudgingly slid aside as the mountain of a man came to the door. "Glad you're here. I see you've met Rieka. She's off-limits. Obviously."

Rieka shot Spike a look that suggested she could set her own limits just fine. Spike met the look with a cheeky wink. Rieka rolled her eyes and turned to go.

"It's a nice night," said Hammond. "Let's take a brief constitutional, shall we?" He plucked his cap from a hook by the door and stuffed it over his unruly hair, his impressive sideburns erupting from under the brim like they were trying to escape to his chin.

"I'm only here to get some directions," Spike began, but before he could finish, the man had a firm hand on his back and was walking him toward the rear of the building.

Spike had always gotten on well enough with Hammond. The guy was a bit old-fashioned—but for a vampire of his generation, a bit old-fashioned was downright progressive. His old tweed waist-coat had been tailored for him by a shop that had shuttered back when England was still on its third George.

"Thought about my offer, have you?" Hammond asked.

"Not exactly," said Spike. "Sorry, mate—I can't keep chasing the same stag forever. You weren't kidding about needing muscle, though, if you're keeping humans on retainer these days." He nodded toward the side door.

Hammond chuckled. "Only *mostly* human. Rieka spends each full moon with a set of fangs that make yours look like baby teeth."

Spike bristled. "No," he said. "Harry Hammond. You? You're the one who taught me that joke about the three werewolves and the imp. You used to go hunting on full moons in the hopes you might get to come home with some fur under your fingernails. Now you're running with a werewolf of your own?"

"I know, I know." Hammond shook his head. "Never would have imagined it in the old days. But you know what the Bard says about miserable times and strange bedfellows. Anyway, she pulls her weight. Tough as tacks, she is. She sorta lets the beast bleed into the beauty. It's there, all the time, just under the surface. Plus, you'd be amazed how useful it is to have someone around who can flit about as she pleases in daylight hours. She looks out for us when the sun is shining, and we return the favor at night."

"Yeah." Spike swallowed dryly and flexed his burned arm. "I can imagine that would be handy." He cleared his throat as they made their way in a lazy stroll around the factory lot. "Speaking of daylight," he said, "I went to Waterloo today. Midday. It didn't go well."

"Pulled a Napoleon?" Hammond asked.

Spike sighed. "More or less." By the time he had finished

recounting the events of the disastrous day, Hammond was nodding soberly, his brow heavy. "Gray suits? Red ties? Yeah, that'd be Gunnar's goons. Told you he was bad news. He's got hundreds of demons on his payroll—every sort you can imagine—Fyarls, M'Fashniks, Slods. Not a lot of holdouts who don't answer to Gunnar these days."

"You seem to know a lot about the bloke. Know where I can find him?"

Hammond regarded Spike soberly for several seconds. "You won't bring him down alone," he said at last. "Trust me. We pulled a payroll heist a few weeks back. Planned the job for weeks. Should've been a sure thing—would've cut off the bastard's resources, weakened his hold on the city, given the rest of us a little breathing room. Instead, two of my crew are dust and my inside man is locked up in Gunnar's private dungeon."

Spike took in a breath through his teeth and shook his head. "Thanks for that. Puts my cock-up in Waterloo into perspective. Does the guild know you're out here pitching rocks at the hornets?"

Hammond rolled his eyes. "The guild is dead. Ruthven and Orlok have been dragging the corpse of the thing behind them for years."

"Only Ruthven now," said Spike. "Apparently Count Orlok's fled the sinking ship. Months ago, according to Ruthven."

Hammond shook his head. "Was only a matter of time. That lot can't even manage their own problems, let alone find the time to come sticking their noses in mine for giving Gunnar what's coming to him. Bastard's got to be dealt with, Spike. Why don't you step inside and we'll talk shop? I hung a stable hand to bleed not half an hour ago. Got him out in Warley. Fresh from a farm."

"Thanks, but I'll pass," Spike said. "Look, the fact is, I've got no problem sharing the streets with a few well-dressed demons. Plenty of beefeater blood to go around. Let him have his reign over the London underworld. I'm not looking to start a war. I just want my haul."

Hammond stared at Spike for several seconds. "You're looking for a bleedin' parley with the Dread Lord of London Town?"

Spike nodded.

Hammond slapped a hand over his face and dragged it away slowly. "You're dreaming if you think that ruddy knuckle is gonna give you a fair shake. Lucky to walk out of that meeting with your head still attached to that skinny neck of yours." He draped an arm over Spike's shoulders. "Listen. You're a hell of a scrapper, Spike. You know we could really use the muscle right now, and it'd be a waste to see you dusted. We're plannin' a jailbreak job to bust my guy out of Gunnar's stronghold. Tell you what. I'll give you twice my usual rate if you help us pull it off—offer goes for your whole gang, if they want in. One night only."

"Because picking a fight with the biggest bully on the playground went so well for you last time." Spike shrugged off the arm and faced Hammond. "I may be a top-shelf terror, but I'm not taking on an entire sodding army because your idiot got pinched. I'm worried about my own crew, and Gunnar happens to have nicked the one thing that might keep it tethered together. Just tell me where I can find him."

Hammond's chest rose and fell as he heaved a heavy sigh. He looked up at the old factory and shook his head. "Fine," he said, finally relenting with a grunt. "I know how it feels, trying to keep a funny old family from falling apart."

A few minutes later, Spike was back on the road with an address in hand.

Take that, Darla. Yesterday had been a mess, sure, but since then he had made a clear and meaningful goal, and he was well on his way to achieving it. He allowed himself a smile as he skipped up the alleyway. By now, Darla was probably back home with Drusilla, assuming the worst about him. She almost certainly would not approve of Spike poking about the premises of such a high-profile individual when they were supposed to be lying low, but he didn't need to tell her every little thing.

Darla, to be fair, did not tell Spike every little thing, either. She had not told him about the ticket, for example, nor about the Master—nor would she ever get around to telling him that just as he was heading toward Gunnar's, she was hanging awkwardly from a drainpipe outside the bedroom window of the British prime minister.

CHAPTER TEN

Darla shifted her grip on the drainpipe, cursing softly under her breath. It had been too much to hope, of course, that Lord Salisbury might have left a window open just a crack to let in the night air. It wasn't as if she could have let herself in, even if he had. Rules were rules, and Darla did not have a formal invitation.

She actually *had* been invited inside 10 Downing Street in the past. Twice, in fact, by two separate prime ministers. Inevitably, though, favor shifted in the House of Commons and the stately home and offices changed hands—nullifying any previous welcome. She tried to mentally tally how many prime ministers had occupied the abode since she last had access to it—seven? Nine? She could never keep up. But she *could* remember where the bedroom was.

This had felt like much more valuable information *before* Darla had discovered that Lord Salisbury was apparently London's soundest sleeper. The heavy blankets rose and fell as rhythmic snores rumbled through the glass. Rapping on the pane and calling out as loudly as she dared proved insufficient, so Darla decided a note would have to suffice. Fine. She had planned for this eventuality, and so she had both paper and a full fountain pen in her purse. Once she was satisfied with her wording, she folded the paper tidily, ready for delivery. But the window still wasn't open.

Darla cursed again and made a fist.

The sound of broken glass tinkling down to the flagstones below was excruciatingly loud. She waited, hoping the noise had escaped the notice of the guards—but a few moments later, a uniformed yeoman appeared around the corner, scanning the area. *Damn.* Darla tossed the letter hastily through the broken pane, feeling the supernatural barrier press back against her fingertips as she released it. Within, the sleeping figure stirred in his bed and grunted. Of course *now* he was waking up.

Shouts erupted from below, and Darla shinnied up the drainpipe, pulling herself over the gutter as the startled guard sounded the alarm. It was fine. She would have preferred a clean drop, but by the time they reached the roof, she would be long gone.

She found herself feeling strangely exhilarated as she brushed her hands off on her dress. She had to admit, she would miss this. She would never confess as much to Spike, but there was something to be said for daring close calls and constantly shifting plans. It felt almost like being alive.

A thick bolt of wood rocketed past her cheek and exploded against a chimney in a spray of splinters. Darla whirled, baring her fangs and dropping into a fighting stance. There was no way that stuffy yeoman had gotten up here so quickly!

A man was standing across from her on the rooftop not twenty feet away. His tunic and trousers were both black, and so was the stupid floppy hat on his head. He held a sleek steel contraption that looked like a crossbow, but instead of standard arrows, it had been scaled up to launch thick wooden stakes as long as a man's forearm. Not taking his eyes off her, he slung the spent weapon over a hook on his hip. He had a bandolier strapped across his chest, studded all over with silver crosses and fitted with glass bottles, iron pendants, and more sharpened stakes. Even in the open air, Darla could smell garlic wafting across the roof. The man plucked a plum-size glass globe out of one of his straps, holding it like a live explosive. Within the bauble, clear water sloshed. Holy water. Darla swallowed. This was *not* a standard yeoman, then. He had to be one of Edward's bloody Blackhearth operatives.

Darla cringed at her own naivete. If Buckingham was so worried about occult attacks, then of course there would be sentinels stationed around *all* the significant figures in London.

"Quite a climb, creature," said the man, melodramatically brandishing the globe. "Allow me to quench your thirst."

From over the peak of the roof, a second man appeared, smaller than the first but clad in the same sable uniform. He surveyed the situation and then drew a crossbow of his own, leveling it at Darla. Two against one. Darla still liked her odds.

"You're going to have to be a much better shot than your friend if you're hoping to hit my heart from that distance," she called. "More liable to just make me mad."

"Don't need a clean shot," called the second operative. "These bolts are laced with Interfector Mortis. Heard of it?"

Darla tensed. *Killer of the Dead.* There weren't many poisons that could bring down the already deceased, but that would get the job done. Painfully, too. How had Blackhearth even gotten their hands on it? He could be bluffing. She watched the man's eyes from over the top of his weapon. He didn't look like he was bluffing.

"Watch yourself, Roddy!" hissed the first operative. "She's one of them! She can get inside your mind, seduce you with her sinful wiles!"

"Seriously?" Darla straightened. "*That's* what you're watching for?"

"Don't play your tricks on me, wanton witch!"

Darla crossed her arms. "I'm an undead creature of the night with superhuman strength, razor-sharp fangs, and three hundred years of practice tearing men like you apart," she said. "And you're worried that my first move would be to *seduce* you?"

The second operative—Roddy—glanced at the first, his crossbow still fixed on Darla. "She's got a pretty good point, Chuck," he said. "She doesn't seem like she trying to seduce anybody."

"Don't listen to her!" snapped Chuck. "She's doing it right now! Can't you feel it? It's mind manipulation!"

Darla rolled her eyes.

"You ever consider that maybe you're just attracted to strong women?" asked Roddy. "And you blame them for your own uncomfortable feelings?"

"Right?" said Darla. "Thank you."

"Enough!" snapped Chuck, and with no further debate, he lobbed the globe at Darla.

She whipped to the right, dodging easily, but she felt a sharp sting as the glass burst against the chimney and several drops sizzled on the back of her neck. With a hiss, she spun and ripped a brick free from the masonry, raising her arm to launch it through the prat's skull.

No. She caught herself at the last second. She couldn't kill the bastards outright. Not only would that make Salisbury much less inclined to agree to a meeting, but eviscerating a pair of Buckingham's best in broad moonlight would instantly exacerbate matters for the vampire community. Stay focused, Darla.

"Look. I haven't killed anybody all night," she said, lowering the brick to her side. "And if you promise not to do anything stupid, it might stay that way."

"You *haven't killed anybody*," scoffed Chuck, "because *we* interrupted your pernicious plot, didn't we?" With that, he plucked another device from his bandolier. This one looked like a tin can fitted with a little plunger on top. He waggled it meaningfully at Darla. "Devil Dust," he declared. "Packed it myself. Silver powder, dried garlic, and wild roses, topped off with a healthy handful of black powder to give the whole thing a kick."

Darla raised an eyebrow. "Why wild roses?"

"Because they . . ." Chuck hesitated. "Because they're . . . bad? For vampires?" He glanced behind him at Roddy, who shrugged. "Never mind the roses!" Chuck's gaze whipped back to Darla. "Eat dust, foul villain!"

He jammed the plunger down and tossed the canister in a high arc over Darla's head. As soon as it was in the air, Chuck stuffed his fingers in his ears. Behind him, Roddy ducked beneath the roof's peak.

Instinctively, Darla pitched the brick. The two projectiles met midair with a dull clank, sending the metal canister spiraling back toward the operative.

Chuck's eyes widened. He threw himself backward just as the explosive went off with a sharp *pop*. In an instant, a glittering cloud of smoke and powder erupted above him. The brick *thunk*ed onto the roof beside Darla, tumbling down the incline and into the gutter. Chuck coughed and covered his face with his arms as he staggered around in a sparkly haze.

Darla seized the opportunity and hurried to the edge of the roof. It was a three-story drop to the flagstones below, but she had landed farther jumps in taller heels.

"Don't!" called the second operative. Darla glanced back. Roddy was approaching, crossbow still leveled squarely at her chest. "We can take you in, or we can scatter you to the wind. I've got a pair of silver-lined manacles on my belt. Come quietly, and I don't have to end you."

Between them, Chuck groaned, rubbing his eyes as he staggered blindly out of the cloud and closer to Darla. "Wossat?" he said. "Of course we gotta end her! Gonna end every last one of the monsters!"

Darla raised an eyebrow.

Roddy gave his partner a long-suffering glare. "Watch where you're going, Chuck," he said. "Stay out of my line of fire."

"Hmm?" Chuck was blinking rapidly and shaking powder out of his hair. He had lost his floppy hat somewhere in the dust, and he smelled like burned garlic bread with floral accents.

Darla threw herself forward before Roddy had time to pull the trigger. In a flash, she caught Chuck from behind, pinning his arms and holding him like a struggling, reeking meat shield between herself and Roddy.

"Unhand me, you sultry wretch!" Chuck grunted. Darla dug her nails into his arms.

Roddy did not lower the weapon.

"Stake through the heart might sound like a special vampire

thing," Darla called to him over her captive's shoulder, "but it works fine on humans, too. Trust me. I've tested it."

"Don't let her turn me into one of them!" yelled Chuck. Darla sneered. She had no intention of putting her lips anywhere near the man's sweaty neck, especially not now that it was all dusted with charred garlic and sparkling with silver flecks, but she tightened her grip anyway, thinking fast. Things were so much easier when you could just eviscerate nuisances and get on with your evening. "She's got me, lad," Chuck said grimly. "I'm done for. Do it. Follow protocol."

"Wait," said Darla. "What?"

Roddy nodded soberly. He squeezed the trigger.

The cord twanged like a bass string, and the heavy bolt whistled through the air. Darla wrenched Chuck back and to the right, and the bolt skimmed the man's lapel before sailing off to shatter a window somewhere in the Foreign Office building across the street.

"Really?" Darla demanded. "It's bad enough I don't get to kill this tosser, but you're actually going to make me *save* him? Am I being punished?"

Roddy was already cocking his crossbow again. He straightened, nocking a second round, and slid closer, closing the gap between them.

"Listen. I think perhaps we've got off on the wrong foot," said Darla. "How about you put down your pointy stick and I put down my quivering hostage, and we all go about our business? Hmm?"

Roddy raised his weapon again. Behind him, an access door flew open and three more men in midnight-black uniforms with ridiculous floppy black hats came trotting out, decked with similar kits. Darla groaned inwardly. Oh, good. Reinforcements. That's what the situation needed. Stakes slid out of holsters, and more crossbow strings tightened.

Darla gritted her teeth and pulled her captive backward a few more steps. Three stories. She could land the jump, but Chuck couldn't—and the moment she let go of her human shield, she was liable to have bolts tipped with Infector Mortis zipping toward her from all angles. Her reflexes had been sharp enough to dodge Roddy's first shot, but she wasn't keen on her chances of dodging them all.

Her foot found the gutter behind her, and she pulled Chuck close. "How well do you think you could survive a three-story fall?" she whispered in his ear.

"Wh-what?" he stammered.

"Never mind," she said. "Just thinking out loud." And then, with both arms tight around the man's chest, she kicked off, and the two of them were coasting backward.

The situation was not ideal.

It wasn't as if Darla had never leaped off a rooftop with a screaming victim before. Once, she had ridden an old lady like a toboggan down several levels of steep tiles.

The difference was that this time Darla was on the bottom.

She did her best to maneuver the flailing idiot as they plummeted, trying to ensure that he didn't land directly on his head—but Chuck was less than cooperative, and Darla didn't have much time to work with. Before she was ready for it, the road slammed into her from behind with a sickening crack, and her vision flashed red and white as the operative landed with a meaty thump on top of her.

Darla allowed herself a moment or two before opening her

eyes. A face poked over the edge of the roof high above her as she did. Her vision was swimming, but it had to be Roddy.

The body on top of her let out a wheezing groan. Not dead? Well, that was something. She would count that as a solid mark in the *success* column. She could feel several bones crunching themselves back into position along her spine as her body healed itself.

The face looking down at her pulled back out of sight for a moment, and she heard Roddy's muffled voice barking a command to the others.

Darla clenched her jaw and pushed herself up, letting Chuck flop limply onto the cobblestones.

By the time Roddy's face reappeared, along with several of his Blackhearth brethren, Darla was already gone.

CHAPTER ELEVEN

An hour after he had left Hammond's place, Spike found himself approaching a towering old building on Wych Street. The whole neighborhood was a relic of a bygone London, with weathered flint cobbles, old-style gables on every building, and stately inns dating back to the fifteenth century. London was funny that way. A hundred cities from a hundred time periods all found themselves stitched together here, so the span of half a block could seem to transport passersby a hundred years if they weren't paying attention. Wych Street was far from idyllic—Spike needed to duck under a clothesline full of well-worn underwear and side-step a lumpy puddle as he neared his destination—but there was no denying that the place had charm. It was a neighborhood that wore the trappings of a common slum like an ill-fitting costume, elegance and class still peeking through every seam.

There was no question the address Hammond had given Spike was correct. It wasn't simply that the building loomed a good two stories higher than its tallest neighbors, it was that the looming felt malicious. This was a building that loomed for the sinister fun of it. Somewhere behind him, a hanging sign creaked in the breeze as Spike approached the front door. Gargoyles peered down at him from the rooftop—a little out of place and overly ostentatious, Spike thought—although he was only mostly certain that the one on the left hadn't just turned its head to follow his approach. He was still reaching for the goat's-head knocker when the broad front door swung open. A figure in a dark suit, a red tie, and an expression that could chill beverages stood within. This was not the demon Spike had met on the street. He was shorter and skinnier, and a pair of ram's horns framed his pale face.

"Please come in," the demon said, gesturing for Spike to enter. "Master Gunnar is expecting you."

"No, he isn't," said Spike.

The demon raised a practiced eyebrow. "You are the vampire called Spike—also known as William the Bloody. Following a lengthy delay in Shadwell, you made poor time up Fleet Street and paused unnecessarily around Chancery Lane. Master Gunnar does not appreciate being kept waiting."

Spike scowled, but he stepped inside.

The place smelled like treated leather and expensive cigars. From the foyer, Spike could see some sort of drawing room off to the left, a wide stained-glass window occupying most of one wall. Directly in front of him was a staircase leading up, a pair of gray-suited sentinels standing guard on either side. Both of them were watching Spike's every move closely. No sooner had the demon doorman latched the front entrance than another door swung open to Spike's right. A broad-shouldered figure ascended from the basement, backlit by the flickering glow of firelight and heralded by the sound of several mournful wails echoing up from below. He was wiping his hands unceremoniously on a black towel.

"Master Gunnar," the doorman said. "Your guest has arrived."

"That'll do, Cricklewood." Gunnar tossed the doorman the towel and turned his attention to Spike. Cricklewood bowed and glided away silently into the house. The so-called Dread Lord of London Town wore an impeccably tailored silk shirt the color of expensive merlot, but its sleeves were rolled up over thick, muscular arms, like a casual workman's. His skin was a vivid red, and half a dozen short dark horns protruded from atop his head like a built-in crown. Behind him, the basement door slowly swung shut, as one last tortured moan tapered off into silence.

"If you're busy," Spike said, "I can come back."

Gunnar looked at the door and smirked. "Just keeping up with my hobbies," he said. "I have time to meet with a slayer killer. Come." Without any further ceremony, he started up the stairwell.

Spike eyed the guards as he slipped past them, but the pair remained at their station. Spike followed their boss upward.

"Your reputation precedes you," Gunnar said, a few stairs ahead.

"Does it?" Spike hurried to catch up. "And yet you're not keeping a bodyguard or two around in case I try something?"

Gunnar glanced back over his shoulder. He looked earnestly amused by the notion. "They'll come when they're needed," he said. "But they won't be needed, will they?"

Spike shrugged. "Met a few of them earlier today near Blackfriars. Can't say we hit it off."

Gunnar chuckled easily, but there was a keen edge to his gaze. The demon had a predator's eyes—like a lion in its prime amused to find a scrawny jackal wandering through its den. "Oh, yes.

Sisseroth mentioned something about that. So that was you? He said he didn't get a good look under the mask."

"Just a misunderstanding," said Spike.

"Accidents happen," said Gunnar flatly. "*Spike*, is it? Good name. I had a brood-cousin called *Spike*. Of course, he was a Hastam demon, like me—had these nasty barbs that came out of his wrists. Sorta like . . . *this*." With a sound like a sharp knife carving a roasted turkey, a metal spear slid out of Gunnar's arm and stopped just shy of Spike's chin. Its shaft was round and smooth, but the tip flattened to a razor-sharp edge on both sides, like a narrow sword blade. From a distance, one might have assumed the demon was holding a polished javelin. "So, you see, the name fit," Gunnar finished. "Funny choice for a half-breed like you, though."

Spike bit his tongue.

"Oh, relax." Gunnar withdrew the blade and turned his back to Spike as he resumed his climb. "I know a lotta demon purists won't play nice with vampires. They look down on your lot. Can't blame 'em. What sort of demon walks around all night wearing a human corpse? Eh? Sounds uncomfortable—but to each his own. I for one don't mind working with you bloodsuckers. Got one or two vamps on staff, in fact. Dirty things, but they can be good for scratching those pesky, hard-to-reach itches."

"Very progressive of you," Spike said evenly.

They continued up the staircase. The wood of the railing was neatly polished, and the carpet under their feet was rich and plush. Gunnar's mansion was everything Spike's dank basement wasn't.

Gunnar stole another glance over his shoulder and must have caught the look in Spike's eyes. "Nice, innit?" he said. "Got character. First time I ever came to London was 1666. I saw this place when I arrived and you know what I said to myself? I said, *I like that building. I like it so much, I'm not gonna burn this neighborhood to ashes.* And then I didn't."

"High praise."

"You had to be there. We burned so many buildings that day, the places we *didn't* burn really stood out. Hell of a shindig. Devil's years only come along once a millennium, after all. Good times. There used to be this funny old man up the way who sold pork pies. I wonder if that guy died horribly. I like to think he did."

"A little before my time," said Spike. "Look, I'm really only here about the relic."

They reached the landing, and Gunnar paused for Spike to catch up. "Relic?"

"That church coach your demons hit today. It was carrying a relic of a prophet. A guy called Agabus."

"Never heard of him." The demon shook his head and resumed walking. The hallway was wide, but Gunnar, built like a silverback, still took up most of it. "You know, I had almost forgotten I ordered that job," he mused. "Haven't even opened the bags since they got back. I just like to kill a few priests from time to time to keep up morale. So what did I get? Skull?"

"Pinkie."

"Hmm." Gunnar looked disappointed. "Valuable?"

"Not by your standards," said Spike. "Rare, of course, but you'd need to pay to get the word out underground if you wanted to sell, then line up a buyer, hire a fence—work, work, work. More trouble than it's worth, if you think about it. I'm sure there were plenty of other goodies to make the rest of the haul worthwhile—but the thing is, my girl had her heart set on that manky old finger. You know how it is."

Gunnar snorted. "I hear you. I toppled an empire for a set of triplets once."

"Exactly. So if it's nothing to you, I'd love to take it off your hands. No hard feelings. You can tell your boy Sisseroth I'm not even mad."

Gunnar finally came to a stop at the end of a wide hallway. The wall ahead of them had been gutted, and a heavy metal hatch, like the door to a bank vault, had been installed. "If the relic's not valuable," Gunnar said, leaning on the hatch, "then why do you care so much about giving it to her?"

The image of a one-way ticket to Germany flashed in Spike's mind. "Personal reasons," he said. "It's not about money. It's about principles."

"A parasite with principles. Love to see it." Gunnar chortled. "Oh, speaking of which. If you don't mind." A bob of his horned head indicated the combination lock in front of him. Eldritch runes adorned the outer ring.

"Of course." Spike turned his back to give Gunnar privacy as the demon spun the wheel. A moment later, Spike heard the telltale clank of heavy tumblers shifting and then the creak of metal.

"Coming?" said Gunnar.

Spike turned back in time to follow the demon through the thick vault door before it closed behind them. It was dim on the other side, but Gunnar turned a squeaky knob on the wall and gaslights began to flicker to life, climbing higher and higher, illuminating what looked like the inside of a tall silo made of some kind of dark brick. Spike stepped toward the brass railing in front of them and looked up. A staircase spiraled up at least four stories with landings every ten feet or so, each one marked with a minia-ture gargoyle leering out over the edge. He peered down. The stairs went another few stories in the opposite direction, too, descending well below ground level.

"I want to show you something," Gunnar said. With no further explanation, he headed toward the steps leading down.

Spike followed, but not too closely. "It's not a cask of amontil-lado, is it?" he asked.

"I like you," said Gunnar, not bothering to look back. "You remind me of a young me. Coming in here all cocksure and expecting to walk away with goods that I've rightfully stolen—it's a wonder you can squeeze yourself into those skinny trousers with the pair you must be packing. I respect the ambition, boy. I really do. A blood rat who knew his place wouldn't have come here tonight. He wouldn't have been able to take on a slayer like you did, either."

"Thanks?" Spike said.

Along the wall on the next landing were a pair of doors made of a dark, lustrous metal covered with complicated etchings. Each had a narrow window set in the center. Spike peeked inside as they passed. A chimplike creature with fire dancing across its skin sat slumped against the corner.

"What is this place?" he asked.

"This," said Gunnar, "is where I keep my trophies. You see, I agree with you. It's not about money. It's about principles. Got to have principles. Someone gets in my way or tries to take what's mine, I have an obligation to show them the inside of one of my special little boxes."

The face behind the next window belonged to a birdlike woman with feathery hair. She clawed at the glass as they passed, and then her lips pulled back as she drew a breath to scream. The inscriptions on the door glowed a soft blue, and no sound escaped the cell.

Gunnar smirked. "Nice, right? Those charms alone cost a fortune. They nullify infernal gifts. Worth every penny." He tapped a sharp fingernail on the glass. "Hey, sweetie. You cozy in there?"

"Some people collect spoons," said Spike.

Gunnar smirked. "From what I hear, you traveled clear to China to find the one person most likely to kill you," he said. "Why'd you do it?"

Spike shrugged. "I like a challenge. And I suppose it beat waiting around for the slayer to come find me someday."

"I respect that." Gunnar nodded. "You see a threat, you can't hide from it. You deal with it. You keep anything after you finished her off? Her weapon? Severed hand? Head in an icebox?"

Spike shook his head. "I was traveling light."

"Shame. The memento is the best bit. After I've dealt with a threat, I like to put it in here. The whole thing, heart still beating and everything. It's a sign of respect, really. I hold all my trophies in the highest regard, you see. They are great, in their way—that's why they have to be mine." Gunnar's eyes locked on Spike's for a moment longer than was comfortable. It was difficult to tell if the demon was boasting or threatening.

The bird woman threw herself violently at her cell door. It made only a muffled *thud*.

"Ah-ah-ah." Gunnar waggled his finger at her, then turned back to Spike. "The charms also keep them from going all dead on me too quickly. That's real handy when I forget to feed someone for a few weeks."

They continued down the stairs in a slow spiral. "We're almost there," said Gunnar, but that much was obvious. Spike stepped from the landing to an uneven stone floor.

This bottom level of the tower housed just one cell, but its door was as wide across as the broad side of a barn. Like the others, the metal was inscribed with glowing symbols. They pulsed steadily, letting out a low thrum. Gunnar waited patiently as Spike stepped up to peer through the window.

At first, it looked like an empty cell—until the whole rear wall shifted. What Spike had taken for drab plaster was in fact the broad, thick flesh of an unthinkably enormous creature, like a colossal worm, writhing slowly but unceasingly in an undulating knot. The cell was far more vast than Spike had realized. The chamber that housed this behemoth must have been carved under the basements of the entire neighborhood. Spike staggered backward a step as the coiled giant's face slid into view, a nightmarish mess of fangs and mandibles. A golden eye larger than Spike's entire head swept past the window.

"You barmy bastard," Spike breathed. "That's an Old One."

"He's called Sorm," Gunnar confirmed, grinning broadly at his guest's visible nervousness. "Fully materialized and corporeal— and a pain in my bright-red backside. Makes the serpent Olvikan look like a garter snake. The Old Ones have this nasty habit of thinking they own the place just because they're primordial pure breeds. No respect for their youngers and betters. Sorm here got in my way."

Spike let out a low whistle. "That brute's gonna have your head, mate—and the rest of you—and probably a good piece of London in the process. You can't possibly hope to contain an Old One."

"And a lowly vampire can't hope to kill a slayer," said Gunnar. "But here we are."

Spike regained his composure and straightened. "Okay. Yours is bigger. You win."

"Always." Gunnar chuckled darkly.

"Very impressive," said Spike. "With top-notch trophies like these, I can't imagine what you'd even do with, say, the shriveled left pinkie of some dead guy. Seems like it would be beneath you."

"I couldn't care less about your worthless relic," Gunnar said.

"That's great," Spike began.

"But—" Gunnar cut him off.

"But?"

"But I've got a policy—it's real simple: If something belongs to me, I don't let it go. Not to you. Not to anyone." He narrowed his eyes as he regarded Spike. "I might, however, be convinced to offer the trinket to a new loyal lackey. You could think of it as a signing bonus. You would still be the slayer killer, but you would be *my* slayer killer."

Spike's jaw tensed. "I'm nobody's lackey."

Gunnar shook his head, amused. "You don't see it yet, Spike, but you've only got three options. Option one: You become a part of my nefarious network, work for me, maybe even let my tailor fit you for a respectable suit in place of those filthy rags. Or option two: You can stay out of my way." The demon gave Spike's burned arm a firm pat as he headed back toward the stairs.

Spike ground his teeth as the pain rippled up his shoulder. "And the third option?" he managed.

Gunnar didn't turn to face him as he plodded up the stairs. "You just saw the third option. Why do you think you got treated to the tour?"

The climb back up the steps was uncomfortably quiet. Briefly, Spike wondered if Gunnar had any intention of letting him leave the tower at all. He remained on edge as they passed the cells of miserable prisoners—but when they reached the landing, the demon unlocked the heavy vault door and held it open with calculated civility as Spike stepped through.

They returned to the foyer in silence. A cold lump rose in Spike's throat as he neared the front door. The image of Drusilla's disappointed face hung in his mind. "You sure you couldn't be convinced to let me have it?" he tried. "I'd owe you one. A favor from a slayer killer's got to be worth something. No? I don't suppose you're interested in porcelain cats? Because I know a guy."

Gunnar gave Cricklewood a nod, and the demon doorman put a hand on the doorknob.

"You don't even want the dusty old thing," Spike grumbled.

"Looking for charity? Go bother a nun," Gunnar told him. "If you think I'm giving out freebies so you can please that loony tart of yours, then you're as crazy as she is."

Spike clenched his fists. The guards in gray were watching him closely from their posts at the foot of the stairs.

"Speaking of which," Gunnar grunted, "you should bring your addled other half with you next time. She sounds fun. Tell her she has my personal invitation. I for one have never been one to mind a girl who's not all there up top, as long as the rest of her's in all the right places, if you know what I mean." He chuckled.

Spike's entire body tightened. "What did you just say?"

Gunnar's eyes flashed with vicious delight. "Cricklewood will see you out."

Spike was still seething nearly an hour later as he pounded his fist on the dingy delivery door of the old Lang Building for the second time that night. It was Hammond himself who finally opened it.

"Well?" the old vampire demanded.

Spike's nostrils flared, and he ground his teeth. "I'm in."

CHAPTER TWELVE

Darla's back had been sore since Downing Street, and her disposition had not been much better. At least she had made contact. Waiting to see if Lord Salisbury responded would be an entirely different sort of pain, but she could be patient. On the divan, she turned another page in her novel and scowled moodily.

"Is your story misbehaving itself?" asked Drusilla.

Darla sighed. "It's fine."

"Is it actually fine?"

"Well . . ." Darla tucked a bookmark between the pages. "The way Stoker writes the sisters is rather insulting, frankly. They're the only female vampires in the book, and they're little more than a schoolboy fantasy—seductive bodies, sharp teeth, no personalities. He never even bothers to give them names. This is precisely why everybody always thinks we're just sex and trouble."

Drusilla considered. "I *do* like sex," she said, "*and* trouble."

"Everybody likes sex and trouble," Darla conceded hotly. "But it's reductive. I mean—sure, the real sisters may not be the most riveting conversationalists, but Marita can be witty when she wants to be. Lesli curated a whole collection of Greek antiquities—a good one, too. Some of her helmets still have the original heads inside. And I think Jennifer knits."

"I met the sisters once," said Drusilla, her eyes drifting up to follow the memory as it floated past. "They let me drink a kitten while we were visiting the castle."

"See?" Darla said. "They have layers. That's all I'm saying."

"Do they win in the end?" said Drusilla. "The vampires in your book?"

"I don't know yet." Darla turned the novel over in her hands. "I hope so. I hate it when the characters you're rooting for don't win."

"I like it best when they win, but terribly," said Drusilla. "Or when they lose, but spectacularly."

"That would explain your taste in companionship," said Darla.

Spike arrived shortly after, kicking muck off his boots as he tromped into the basement.

Darla spared him a glance over the top of the book and went back to reading in silence.

"Where have you been, my pet?" Drusilla asked, gliding up to him.

"Sorting a few things out," Spike answered. "I've got a plan."

Drusilla grinned hopefully. "Tell me?"

"We're gonna snatch that sodding relic right out from under Gunnar's nose, army of demons be damned."

Drusilla's smile widened. "How?"

Spike hesitated. "Still working on the details."

"That means he has no plan," said Darla.

"Okay. Maybe *plan* wasn't exactly the right word," admitted Spike. "But I've got an *intent*, and it is solid."

"This is going to end badly," said Darla.

"Hey, now," Spike protested. "I *always* make things work in the end."

"You make *nothing* work."

"Exactly!" said Spike. "When we've got *nothing* going for us, *I'm* the one who makes that nothing *work*. That's what I do."

"It's times like these when I really wish I had got Drusilla a pet instead of letting her sire you."

"I'll have a proper plan," Spike said. "You'll see. And it's not gonna be some petty smash-and-grab job, either. We're putting together a proper caper this time. Full crew."

"No." Darla dropped the book in her lap with a thump. "I am *not* helping you dig your way out of any more idiotic messes. You failed. Damage done. Move on."

"Wasn't asking *you*," Spike snapped. "For your information, I have friends of my own who are gonna help us pull this off."

"You have friends now?"

"In low places. Yeah."

"Name three people who wouldn't sell you to trolls for trolley fare."

Spike bristled. "Read your bloody book."

The following night, a clock in the distance chimed three as Spike and Drusilla made their way through foggy streets and under an overcast sky. Drusilla wrapped her hands around Spike's arm as they walked. She was humming quietly to herself, a tune Spike didn't recognize, but the cadence was cheery and soothing. She was in a good mood—a hopeful mood. There was nothing Spike would not do to keep Drusilla happy.

The trip through Shadwell felt much shorter than it had the last time Spike had come. Hammond's bristly face met them at the door of the Lang Building, and he eagerly welcomed them inside.

The building looked sturdier from within than it did from without, but there were telltale signs of rot and mildew along the walls. The air tasted like ash and paint thinner as they passed an office with cobwebs dancing in the windows. Shortly, they made their way into a wide main room with a high vaulted ceiling. There were several rows of rusty sewing machines in the space, workbenches covered in dust, and a mechanical monstrosity that took up the whole back wall. A faded conveyor belt ran along the length of the old machine, dented wire bins on either side. Spike blinked. Within each of the bins were what appeared to be piles of tiny limbs, dismembered torsos, and wee severed heads with chubby little cheeks. But no blood.

Right, Spike mumbled to himself. *Toy factory.*

A fine layer of dust coated everything in the place.

Toward the back of the room was a rack of baby dolls in various states of assembly. Some were lacking legs, and most still had featureless faces—the paint marked for coloring their pudgy cheeks had long since dried out without fulfilling its purpose—but a few of them were whole. Some were even dressed up like miniature lords and ladies, although these were no less eerie than their incomplete counterparts.

Drusilla breathed in her surroundings. "I like it here," she said. "The air tastes like children's nightmares."

"Thank you for noticing." Hammond beamed at her.

Rieka the werewolf sat atop one of the battered workbenches, eyeing Spike and Drusilla keenly as they entered.

Across from her, a vampire in a ragged waistcoat and a derby was slouching with his back against a support pillar, picking something out of his fangs with a dirty fingernail. His vest looked two sizes too small, and if his hat had ever been buffed, it had been with a rusty wire brush. The guy was squalor in a suit—and yet there was a gleam in his eyes like the edge of a cut-throat razor.

The last figure in the room was a petite woman in a fine high-necked gown who looked jarringly out of place in the squalid surroundings. She was perched with refined posture on a chair in front of one of the dilapidated sewing machines, waiting patiently. Everything about her seemed carefully cultivated to convey the sense that she was tactfully *not* reprimanding you for using the sorbet spoon for your soup, but that the faux pas had been noted and would be held against you in the future.

"Well," said Hammond. "Meet the family."

Spike looked from face to face in the dim factory. "Is this it?"

The shabby vampire stopped picking his teeth long enough to glare moodily at Spike.

Hammond drew up beside Spike and let out a heavy sigh. "We had a full score of experienced vamps only a handful of months ago. They're all either dust or deserters now. Lost two more only last week, and Slick Icky's in the wind. So, yeah. This is it."

Drusilla's gaze found a mote of dust spiraling in the air above her. She followed it, mesmerized, as it spun and twirled.

Hammond tucked his thumbs in the pockets of his vest and turned to address his crew. "All right, you lot," he boomed. "The vampires standin' in your miserable midst are the genuine article. No doubt you've heard of the sinister sister Drusilla and the one and only William the Bloody. Or—sorry—is it just Spike these days?"

Spike shrugged. "Lot's happened in the last few years. Maybe time for a new moniker. *Slayer of slayers*? *Slayer slayer*? Never mind. That's rubbish. Better in my head. *Spike* is fine." He glanced again across the motley assembly. "I would say I'm pleased to meet you all, but, well. Look at you."

"Some of us have already met," the vampire in the tatty derby growled.

"Have we?" Spike narrowed his eyes. The guy reeked of sweat and dried blood. Sloppy eater. Not Spike's preferred crowd.

"Watch yer tone, Mucker," Hammond snapped, pointing a finger as thick as a sausage at the thug. "They're here on my invite, which means they're my guests. You all know what happens to any damn fool on my payroll who disrespects a guest, yeah?"

There were general mumbles of confirmation around the room. "Good. Well you can forget all that—because what *usually* happens is nuffin' compared to what Spike the ruddy slayer killer is likely to do to ya. An' I will stand back and watch him do it. Understood?"

Heads nodded silently.

"That's the spirit," Spike said, rubbing his hands. "We're gonna have loads of fun. Thick as thieves. As thick as literal, actual thieves, in fact, if everything goes according to plan." He eyed Mucker. "Some thicker than others."

"You sure about this, boss?" Mucker mumbled. "I've seen his idea of fun. Him and that sadistic girlfriend of his basically tore my last crew apart when the job was done."

Drusilla giggled, her eyes still tracing the speck through the air.

"Oh!" Spike snapped his fingers. "Oh! Yes! Now I remember you! Didn't recognize you with your legs on! Really pulled yourself together, mate. Good for you." He chuckled softly. "Good times. How's old Patchy doing these days? Ever find his eye?"

Mucker bared his fangs, and his muscles tensed.

"Oh, let it go." Spike waved him off. "Your lot never could take a joke. Besides, you started it."

Mucker snarled through his fangs, clenching and unclenching his fists. "We don't need them, Hammond," he growled. "I've been inside Gunnar's mansion. I've seen the locks. We can handle the security on our own."

"Don't need *us*?" Spike countered, raising an eyebrow at Mucker. "And what exactly do *you* bring to the table? Other than questionable odors and stains old enough to join the Foreign Legion?"

"That's enough." Hammond positioned himself between the two vampires. "Nobody here is in a position to get picky about the company we're keeping. Mucker's got his faults, but he can also defuse a combination arcane lock in five minutes flat. Can you do that?"

"I can mix an old-fashioned-and-blood in under two," Spike said.

Mucker sneered at him.

"You already met Rieka, our resident lycan," Hammond continued. "Girl can lift a carriage horse with her bare hands, and she only gets tougher the closer we get to the full moon."

Rieka cracked her neck and leaned back on the workbench.

"And finally, there's Ed. Short for Edith." Hammond nodded toward the slip of a woman in the high-necked gown. Up close, her skin looked faintly waxy, and her eyes were an unnaturally bright pale blue. "Kukla demon," Hammond continued. "She does this fun trick where she can project her mind into inanimate objects."

Ed stood and gave a modest curtsy.

"You mean like possessing the dead?" Spike said, perking up. "Army of zombies sort of thing? Now we're talking! I don't generally savor working with demons, but off the top of my head, I can think of three . . . four . . . *five* different ways we could use a zombie army right now. *Six* if you can get them to talk."

"Not that sort of inanimate," clarified Hammond. "More like teapots and bricks. She fancies porcelain dolls best, though."

"It's easier to look through something when it's got a face," the demon added primly.

"Right." Spike's smile faltered. "Army of porcelain dolls. Okay. That's . . . less great. Still, it's got a sort of creepiness factor. We can work with that."

"Only one doll at a time," Ed corrected. "And I can't animate them. I just see what they see."

Hammond gestured at the dusty shelves of forgotten toys. "Ed's our eyes on the outside. She nips her mind into a doll, we tuck it somewhere nearby, and then Ed can see and hear everything that it can. Her body sorta goes limp, and she sits there, all peaceful like, telling us anything we need to know that the doll sees. It's like she's talking in her sleep."

Spike nodded, considering. "And if something gets between you and the doll?"

"My connection stays strong, even from a distance," Ed answered proudly, but then she swallowed. "I simply need to see myself again in order to hop back into my own body. Otherwise it can take days to find my way back to my own mind."

"Right. And until then, your body remains . . . ?"

"Vulnerable," admitted Ed.

Spike turned to Hammond. "If you were bent on diversifying your personnel, you *do* know there are demons who can blow up people's heads from the inside or take a cannonball to the chest, right?"

"Not in a position to get picky," Hammond reminded him.

"I think I'd enjoy being a teapot," mused Drusilla, more to herself than the group.

"Okay," said Spike. "Let me be sure I'm up to speed: We've to somehow get past a fleet of demon thugs, crack a combination arcane lock, and bust a captured demon out of the most secure demonic stronghold in the United Kingdom—and, aside from Dru and me, all we're working with is the saddest excuse for a vampire this side of Sussex, a human who can't stop herself from turning into a sodding *wolf* once a month, and a fragile scrap of a demon whose only power makes her even *more* vulnerable when she uses it. Anything I missed?"

Ed looked like she wanted to argue, but she sat back down instead, her brow furrowed and her lips pursed. Mucker examined his shoes.

Drusilla, meanwhile, had gradually begun wandering toward the bins of baby dolls, running her fingers along the dusty mechanical arms of the machine as she went.

"Ermack," said Rieka.

"Come again?" Spike said.

"Oh, just call him *Ears* like everyone else," Mucker grumbled.

"He's a Kakophonos demon," Rieka continued. "Ermack can control sound—make the dropping of the smallest pin sound like cannon fire or muffle the loudest explosion into a breath of wind."

"Okay, that's a bloke we could actually use," said Spike. "Powers like that are tailor-made for pulling a covert job. Where's Ears?"

"Ears *is* the job," Hammond said. "He's the one Gunnar has locked up in his stronghold."

"Right." Spike pinched the bridge of his nose. "Of course he is. Okay. If we do manage to slip inside undetected, do we know where, exactly, we would even find this Kakophonos demon of yours? Gunnar has a lot of cells and dungeons, and I doubt we're gonna want to take our time checking them all one by one."

Rieka looked grim.

"So that's a no."

Hammond scratched his neck, and for a few moments, no one spoke.

"Got yourself in trouble now, haven't you?" Drusilla's voice broke the silence. She was kneeling next to the machine, peering through the bars of one of the wire bins at a particularly morose looking doll's head. "Were you naughty?" She leaned in closer and whispered: "Were you *going to be* naughty?"

The roughest beginning of an idea fluttered to life at the back of Spike's mind, uncertain and trembling as it flittered forward like a lonely, injured bat trying to flap its way through a labyrinth.

Ed stood and smoothed her dress. "I'm going to put the kettle on," she declared.

"This again?" Mucker tossed his hands in the air. "Lucifer's beard! We're planning the most dangerous heist of our afterlives, and you're leaving to make tea!"

"She has a thing about teatime," Hammond explained, but Spike wasn't paying attention.

"You're a demon!" Mucker hollered after Ed. "And it's the middle of the night!"

Ed spun and addressed him with her chin held high. "If I'm to be keeping nocturnal hours with you decrepit creatures of the night, I will still take tea at four o'clock," she declared hotly. "I may be an abomination, but I'm an English abomination." With that, she stormed out of the room.

Hammond scratched his chin. "I know it's not an ideal team," he said, "but we're all we've got. And more to the point, we're all Ears has got."

"Is he really all that important to you?" asked Spike.

Rieka crossed her arms and fixed him with a steely glare.

"He's on the crew," said Hammond simply. "*My* crew. There's not a wretch in this building hasn't been abandoned. Left lost and alone."

Spike's jaw tightened.

"Well, that doesn't happen to my crew," Hammond continued. "They can bicker and spit all they like—they don't have to like one another—but they don't get left behind."

Rieka drew a deep breath and turned away to pace the floor of the factory.

"Okay." Spike nodded. "So, what's the plan?"

"I was thinking the old Barnabas Grift might be our best play."

"No. Not a chance." Spike shook his head. "We'd need at least two more vamps and a live swan."

"Got a better idea?"

Spike's brow wrinkled as he thought. "How long until the next full moon?"

Rieka ceased her pacing and glanced back. "Week and a half," she answered.

Spike nodded. "And how much brass do you think we could scratch up in a hurry?"

"I could call in some debts," said Hammond. "Lot of folks got my name in their ledgers. Couple hundred pounds by the end of the week?"

"That's a start." Spike pursed his lips. "Not a *great* start, but it's a start."

"Be honest," Mucker grunted. "We're in trouble, aren't we?"

"Not yet," Spike said. "But we will be."

"What're you thinking?" Rieka asked.

"I think," said Spike, "we're gonna need to be naughty."

CHAPTER THIRTEEN

Rieka leaned her palms on the cold roofing tiles and looked out over the quiet city. Several stories below, the bloodsuckers were tucked away, hiding, waiting for her signal. She didn't trust Spike *or* Drusilla, but if she was being honest with herself, she almost preferred it that way. It was easier when they weren't trustworthy. Less of a letdown when they inevitably turned on you. Or got themselves grabbed. She allowed her gaze to drift over the neighborhood, out toward the docks and a boat that wasn't there.

Rieka hadn't always been a lone wolf. Her pack was once everything to her. Baden had called the shots, Minna at his side. Rieka would have followed those two into the burning heart of the sun. There had been nine of them altogether, making their way from city to city. The pack had taught Rieka who and what she was, taught her to understand the wolf within her, to run *with* it, not *from* it. They had been her family.

They would never stay in one town for too long. They traveled by boat, for the most part, forever drifting from place to place. By the time the moon was nearly full, the pack would leave one city for the next, always stopping off in the countryside in between to stretch their legs and wet their fangs. When the moon began to wane, they would pull into the next town. Baden and a few of the others would look for temporary work along the docks—mostly to keep up appearances—while the rest of the pack would fan out into the city. Minna taught Rieka how to grift and shill—and when that didn't work, how to cut purse strings. She also taught Rieka how to throw a punch and how to run. Throw the punch well, and you had plenty of time to do the running. Throw it *very* well, and you didn't have to run at all.

One evening, however, Rieka could neither fight nor flee. There had been too many of them. It had been the pack's last night in London, and she had gotten greedy, hoping for one more big catch before they raised anchor. She was supposed to be back on the boat by sundown—but Rieka had been forced to hide and wait instead, stuck inside a barrel of dried beans. It had seemed like a clever escape at the time, but then the men she had robbed kept hanging around, talking and grumbling in the street for what felt like hours. By the time she had been able to push off the lid and peek out, the sky had turned a rusty burnt orange.

Rieka had raced across London then, dodging past lamplighters and cutting off carriages, her feet barely touching the cobblestones as she hurried for the boat. The sky was already blue-black by the time she reached the waterfront. Her pockets were jingling, at least, and she had hardly been able to wait to see the look on Baden's face when he saw her haul.

But the boat was gone.

She hadn't believed it at first. She paced up and down the river.

They would come back, she told herself. Obviously, they would come back.

Six years later, Rieka was still waiting.

Sitting atop the chilly rooftop now, she felt the same dull ache in her gut that she had felt back then. It had not gotten any smaller, but Rieka had grown around it.

Her pack had abandoned her.

Her first full moon in the city had nearly been disastrous—it had been even *more* disastrous for an unfortunate bay horse stabled in a nearby neighborhood in Hackney. She had gotten out of that mess by the skin of her teeth—thanks more to luck than cunning—but she learned quickly to be wary, to trust no one, and to look out for herself as if nobody was coming for her. Because they weren't.

Rieka shook off the thought and stretched her neck from side to side. She could see her breath in the chilly London air. How long had she been perched on this godforsaken iceberg? If she had been calling the shots, they would have pulled the job already, not spent the past week shinnying up gutter spouts like stray cats. It was torture. She let out a puff of air, watching the cloud fade away in front of her. On the other hand, if the plan worked, it would all be worth it. Ermack's accommodations, she reminded herself, were sure to be far less comfortable.

Rieka looked behind her over the rolling landscape of chimneys and gables. She had first met Ermack less than a mile from here. She allowed herself the faintest smile at the memory. She had woken up that morning in a strange man's bed, covered in his blood, startled out of a peaceful sleep by the screaming of the guy's . . . wife? Girlfriend? Maid? Rieka hadn't hung about to ask. She had grabbed some clothes and hightailed it out of there. Normally, London was good about minding its own business, but apparently the whole damn building had been full of people who cared about that dead bastard, because they gave chase. Rieka had a proper mob on her heels by the time she hit the Strand. She thought she might have finally lost them as she pelted down a backstreet, but then a stranger came barreling around the corner toward her from the opposite direction. Rieka had frozen, waiting for the man to try to grab her. He had halted in his tracks, panting and eying Rieka nervously. In the cool moonlight, his skin had been a pale lavender.

After a few seconds, he had straightened up. "You, too?" he said.

Before Rieka could reply, a red-faced man skidded into the street behind him and barked a furious "I got him!"

The lavender stranger barely had time to turn before he was grabbed by the lapels and nearly lifted off his feet. His pursuer shoved something into his face, muttering in what sounded like Latin. Rieka heard a hiss like water boiling over onto a hot stove, and the struggling stranger yelped.

Rieka's body acted on instinct. She felt her fist smash into the new man's rosy cheekbones before she realized what she was doing, and he went over backward like a sandbag. She glanced up at the stranger. He had a fresh burgundy scar burned into his cheek. It looked like an X—no, a cross—just below his eye. The sounds of shouts and footsteps were getting closer, and Rieka couldn't tell which side of the street they were coming from. The stranger wrapped an arm over her shoulders and yanked her into a narrow alleyway.

There, they hid behind a rubbish bin, pressing themselves close together to stay out of sight. The angry voices grew louder, and soon the street was full of people. Rieka was panting, her heart pounding like cannon fire. There was no way they wouldn't be caught.

Gently, the stranger pressed a finger to his lips, and Rieka's breathing became silent. She could still feel her lungs filling and emptying, but not the faintest sound escaped. He peeked over the edge of the bin and gestured with one hand at the alley on the opposite side of the street. Suddenly, Rieka could hear something over the din of voices—a scrabbling, shuffling sound. "Over there!" Someone barked, and the procession pressed into the far alley in pursuit of the noise.

She would learn later that the stranger had put a dome of silence around them both and then amplified the noise of some passing rodent to draw the mob's attention. When the crowd had gone, he finally took his arm off of Rieka's shoulders and stood. The sound of her heartbeat returned.

"Hello," he said. His voice was soft. "Ermack. Demon, second circle. You?"

Rieka could have lied. She could have run. She could have allowed her survival instincts to shield her. Instead, her head swimming, she told him the truth.

She hadn't expected the words to feel so heavy. Outside of her pack, Rieka had never told another soul about the wolf. When she was done, Ermack simply nodded in approval and wiped a bit of dried blood off her cheek with his thumb. "Do you like lamb?" he asked. "I know a place. Very fresh."

They had met a few more times that month, and Rieka found herself floating after every meeting. It wasn't just the red meat, although that didn't hurt. She had not been honest with someone in ages; it felt as if she had pulled out a splinter that had been buried deep inside her chest for so long, she had forgotten what life felt like without it. She was still hesitant, not eager to trust anyone with her whole heart, not ever again, but Ermack did not rush her.

One full moon, she had made her way to a quaint farm on the outskirts of the city, as she had done countless times. The last thing she remembered before releasing the wolf was the smell of hay rolling in off of a broad field, and a weathered chicken coop before her. When she awoke, however, there were brick buildings all around her and a coppery taste in her mouth. She was wrapped in a thick coat and someone was carrying her. Groggy and exhausted, she willed her eyes to focus. It was Ermack.

She cursed her carelessness. She hadn't gone far enough, and the wolf, ever hungry for more substantial prey, had bounded back into the city. Not merely the city, but Rieka's own neighborhood. It was reckless enough to hunt where you might be found, but it was another thing entirely to do so where the people who found you were sure to recognize you. Ermack had heard the cries and pieced together what had happened. He discovered Rieka collapsed from the exertion, covered her up, and carried her stealthily away from the scene of the massacre before anyone else could stumble upon her.

He had come for her.

Swaddled in a cozy bundle in his arms, rocking with the rhythm of his footsteps, Rieka had stared up at that pale purple face, unable to look away.

Ermack had not let her be taken then, and he would not have let her waste away in some paranormal prison.

Rieka flexed her hands. Her fingertips were starting to feel numb. She pulled out her pocket watch and checked the time. If the past week of freezing her tail off on rooftops had been worth it, then a pair of ugly mugs in red ties should be coming around the corner any minute now. They had better make their appearance tonight, or Rieka would be stuck in surveillance purgatory for another week.

A movement caught her attention, and she squinted into the gloom. It was a ragged old man, rummaging through bins a block away. Rieka silently hoped he found something good. She had dug through her fair share of rubbish in this stinking city.

Petty theft was well and good if you were going to be gone by the end of the month, but it was often more risk than reward if you planned to stay put. Rieka had found legitimate work where she could, but something always went wrong. She would miss a shift without explanation, murder a foreman, get her clothes caked in mud and blood. It was so hard to be a professional woman and also a wolf.

It wasn't much better for Ermack. The smaller hordes were all consolidating under the syndicate banner, and Ermack was done serving vainglorious overlords. He had spent too many centuries in hell being used as a glorified megaphone for demons like Gunnar, and now that he had moved out of the seven circles and into the overworld, he wasn't about to volunteer. He was his own demon.

Rieka found a prospect with a local coven, but the witches wouldn't allow Ermack to stay, and every full moon they would have required Rieka to be chained in the basement. She couldn't betray the wolf like that. Or leave Ermack out in the cold. They were the only two companions who had stuck with her through thick and thin.

And then there had been Harry Hammond. The old vampire was a little rough around the edges, and the jobs he ran were never easy or clean—but he had work for them if they wanted it, and he paid what he owed. They made no commitments. They could leave if they wanted to and murder whom they pleased, so long as they tidied up after. Rieka liked that. Hammond gave them a roof to live under and a surrogate pack of degenerates to call a family.

The real test, of course, had been Ermack getting grabbed. It was Rieka's fault. She had let the wolf take over too much of her mind, lost herself in the moment, and forgotten the plan entirely when it mattered most. She had raced after a fleeing demon like an idiot pup chasing rabbits—and so she hadn't been in position when Ermack needed her. Rieka had nearly torn Hammond's throat out when the big vampire had stopped her from rushing back in. Hammond had been right, of course—Rieka getting herself killed would not have spared Ermack any strife. She might have torn through Hammond anyway, had he not been firm and clear about one thing. He said it over and over: They were going to get Ermack back.

Rieka forced her mind to return to the job at hand. Four stories below her, a pair of gray shapes finally turned the corner, red neckties gleaming like bull's-eyes on their chests. If she didn't know any better, she might have mistaken them for humans from this distance. She glanced at her watch. Right on schedule.

No more waiting. Time to act.

CHAPTER FOURTEEN

Spike clicked his own pocket watch shut and watched the street anxiously. The building before them was not Gunnar's mansion. That phase of the plan would come soon enough, but certain ducks had to be put into certain rows first. There were no signs hanging over the shop's nondescript door, nor even any windows at eye level. It was the sort of place that did not need to advertise, because the people who might need to know about it already knew and the people who didn't know about it were surely happier that way. Any advertisement accurate enough to do the shop justice would have given the local schoolchildren nightmares.

"Get ready," he whispered. "Any minute now."

In the shadows behind him, Drusilla leaned closer. "You're sure we can't kill anyone?" she whispered. "Not even a little bit? I like the killing part best."

"You know I do too, love," Spike said. "But we're trying a little finesse this time. Might be fun. I'll take you out for a nice homicide in the country after, to celebrate."

"With torture on top?"

"Of course." Drusilla smiled and bit her lower lip. Spike pressed his forehead against hers. "You deserve it," he whispered.

"Could you two wait to get all horny and horrifying until *after* we've pulled this off?" Rieka whispered, landing in a crouch on the paving stones behind them. "Or not at all? That would be fine, too."

Spike shot her a glare. "Well?" he said.

Rieka gave him a solemn nod.

She was all no-nonsense, that one—but at least she was taking the job seriously. It had been over a week since the ordeal at Waterloo, and Spike was not having a repeat of that disaster. This time it would be different. The whole team had planned and practiced their parts until they could recite their roles in their sleep.

"All right, then. Curtain up. Let's start the show," he whispered. Their window of opportunity would be small, but they only needed a few minutes for this to work. "Stick close."

Spike slipped from his hiding place and hurried up to the quiet building. He glanced left and right, then took a running leap, kicked off the wall, and caught hold of the eaves hanging over the second floor. He pulled himself up into the shadows of the overhang, and a muffled whoosh behind him announced that Drusilla had followed suit.

Rieka's footsteps were thunderous by comparison, but she kept up as stealthily as she was able, pressing her back against the wall once she had crossed the street. A canvas satchel hung across her chest. "A little help?"

Spike reached down, and Rieka jumped to grab hold of his hand. He hoisted her up until her boots found traction on the ledge of the solitary second-story window.

"You two are pretty smooth," Rieka whispered. "I wonder why we don't hear about more vampire burglars."

Spike sighed. "I think we're more suited to highway robbery and good old-fashioned back-alley murders. Got the treacle?"

Rieka pulled a jar from her satchel and waggled it at him before popping off the lid. "But why is that, do you think? You're quiet as cats, you've got extraordinary muscle control, and your night vision must be wicked." Using a rag from her back pocket, she began to smear the sticky black syrup over the glass.

"Sure." Spike kept an eye on the road while she worked. "Not to brag, but we also possess a profound lack of respect for other people's property and a dark void where our morality should be— which is pretty great, I know. It's the whole *needing to be invited into the building that we intend to burgle* thing that tends to throw a spanner in the works."

"Right." Rieka nodded. "Forgot. Sorry. So, how does that rule work, exactly?" Having coated the windowpane to her satisfaction, she flattened out the rag and pressed it snuggly against the sugary mess until it was more or less glued into place.

"You know how it works," Spike said. "We can't cross the threshold uninvited. Big nasty powers come with big nasty limits."

"Do those limits include demon-owned properties?"

"Usually," Spike confirmed. "Some exceptions. Luckily, our man Gunnar gave Dru and me his own personal invitation to his place on Wych Street, so we're covered. Wasn't that thoughtful of him?"

Rieka seemed to consider for a moment. "What if someone had just cleared ground where a house was *going* to be? I assume you could still walk across that, yeah? So when does it start keeping you out? Could you enter if it was still only a frame with no doors or walls?" Rieka capped the jar and wiped her fingers off on her grubby jumpsuit.

"Sure. Not a proper building yet. Could we stick to the task at hand?"

Rieka balled her hand into a fist and held her breath. The blow produced only a muffled crunch. As planned, the shards clung to the sticky fabric, flopping with the rag into a crunchy lump on the sill rather than raining down on the paving stones like chimes. Rieka gingerly snapped off a few stubborn edges, then reached inside and opened the latch. "What about a gazebo? Could you enter a finished gazebo?" she asked.

"Obviously," whispered Spike. "Don't be stupid."

"Remember when we ate that couple snogging under a gazebo?" Drusilla recalled wistfully. "Where was that?"

"Stockholm," said Spike. "That was a nice night. Romantic. Great view over the water. Those kids had excellent taste."

The window squeaked faintly in protest as Rieka slid it open. "How about a veranda with a screen all around it?" she pressed as she lowered herself into the dark room. "Could you enter one of those? Or a tent—could you break into a tent uninvited?"

"I wouldn't know. I've never tried to enter a tent, invited or not, because I'm neither a backwater rube nor a hungry bear. Could we try to focus?"

Rieka's boots made a quiet *thud-thud* as they hit the floor, and then there was silence.

"We should do handsy handful," whispered Drusilla while they waited.

"No killing," Spike reminded her. "Besides, they're not gonna fall for handsy handful."

"But it's fun. I love when you do handsy handful." Drusilla stuck out her bottom lip. "We could try it without the killing."

Spike glanced at his pocket watch. "Nearly time." He slipped onto the window ledge and peered into the darkness. The room was full to brimming with arcane antiquities, vials of rare poisons, and various magical artifacts. Rieka's face popped back into view right in front of him. "Well?" he said. "Let's go."

Rieka reached toward him to help herself up, and he instinctively tried to offer his hand in return, but it halted midair as if the windowpane was still whole and firm. He shook his wrist irritably.

"Do I have to do everything this phase?" Rieka muttered. She hopped up on a table and used a set of nearby shelves to leverage herself up to the windowsill. Behind her, a black vase teetered precariously on its shelf.

Spike sucked in a breath through clenched teeth as the vase tipped—but Rieka's reflexes were sharp. Holding on to the ledge with one hand, she caught the vase with the other, setting it gingerly back in place. A moment later, she was squeezing herself and her canvas bag back out through the window.

"Careful with that thing." Spike nodded toward the satchel. He could see the slight lump outlining a shape no bigger than a loaf of bread. With one last glance at his pocket watch, he dropped to the paving stones below. "Toss it down to me," he whispered. "We haven't got much time before—"

But before he could say it, the first dark figure slid out from around the corner. Against the fog hanging over the street, the demon was a silhouette in gray with just a streak of red where the bright color of his necktie cut through the gloom.

"Bollocks," groaned Spike. The satchel landed in his open arms with a *whump*.

A second demon joined the first, and this one Spike recognized. In addition to the standard outfit, he had round tinted spectacles and a pair of obsidian horns that peeked out from the waves of his black hair. Sisseroth. Together, the demons advanced.

Spike looked up at Rieka, who was frozen on the windowsill. Drusilla remained perched in the shadows of the eaves. She mimed eviscerating the guards, but Spike shook his head almost imperceptibly before turning his attention to the matching minions. He rubbed the back of his neck.

"Spike?" The bespectacled demon clicked his tongue as he neared. "You can't possibly be this stupid, can you?" The demon's voice was a rasping hiss.

"You'd be surprised." Spike shifted the bundle behind his back. "Sisseroth, right? Mind if I call you Sissy? I hope you know you look like a pillock with those glasses on at night."

"And you look like you don't listen very well."

"What—you mean this?" Spike glanced behind him at Rieka, who, in the manner of anyone who has ever been caught on a windowsill trying to look less conspicuous, was only managing to look more so. "Well," Spike said, "to be fair, you're not supposed to come around that corner for another forty-five seconds, so whose fault is it, really? Hmm?"

"Hand over the goods." Sisseroth gave his associate a nudge, and the second demon stepped forward, cracking his knuckles, his human disguise dropping to reveal a face full of spines. He looked like a durian and had a stench to match.

"Wait, I get it. Is this street part of your syndicate's territory?" Spike asked innocently. "I had no idea. This seemed like such a quaint little infernal imports shop. I couldn't resist. Tell you what, let's just pretend this pretty trinket we nicked is for your boss." He brought the satchel out from behind his back. "Call it a gift to show him there's no bad blood."

Durian Face snatched the bag out of Spike's hands and passed it to his partner.

Sisseroth peeked inside and raised an eyebrow. "I knew you were into some weird stuff . . . but really?"

"It's a rare, haunted item," said Spike. "Priceless. Evil. Right up Gunnar's alley. Honestly, I think he'll be delighted."

Sisseroth closed the satchel and shrugged. "Maybe. We're still gonna have to take you in. You can try to run if you want. You won't get far."

"Right, of course," said Spike. He scowled and swayed on his feet. "Whoa. Wait a minute."

"Whatever you're trying, it's not going to work," grunted Sisseroth.

Spike put out a hand and caught Durian Face by the shoulder. "Oof. Hang on, mate," he said. "No, really—a solid hold, if you don't mind. Feeling a bit dizzy here."

"You . . . *want* me to grab you?" the demon asked.

"If you don't mind."

The demon turned to Sisseroth, who shrugged. "Okay." He locked his hands around Spike's arm.

Spike leaned into Durian Face's grip—and not a moment before his legs began wobbling like a baby deer. "I knew I shouldn't have touched that thing," he mumbled. Sisseroth looked at the satchel in his hands again, nervously. Abruptly, Spike's knees buckled, and he clutched at Sisseroth with his other hand to stop himself from falling. The two demons suddenly found themselves supporting the vampire's entire weight between them. "Don't drop me," Spike wheezed.

"Oh, for the love of—" Sisseroth growled, but he was cut off as a flurry of black and red swooped through the air above him, and then Drusilla's heels were suddenly driving themselves into his chest.

Sisseroth fell backward, and as he did, Durian Face was wrenched to the ground with him, clutching his collar and making a noise like a large, angry goose with a much smaller goose stuck in its throat. Spike straightened and dusted off his hands.

Rieka hopped down to the sidewalk as both demons clawed at their own throats frantically. Their bright-red neckties were knotted tightly to each other, and each time one of them tugged at theirs to free themselves, the other lurched and gagged. Spike stood over them. "You two," he said, "just fell for handsy handful. That's embarrassing for you. Now if you don't mind, I'll have that bag back."

He stooped to snatch the satchel, but Sisseroth clung to it, tightening his grip. As Spike pulled harder, the canvas tore in two, and out tumbled a glassy-eyed baby doll in a pink dress and white lace. Spike made a grab for it, but Sisseroth was faster. Durian Face made a gurgling noise as his partner's lunge yanked the tie even tighter. His whole head was turning purple, spines and all.

"Leave it!" Rieka yelled. "We need to go!"

Spike pursed his lips, hesitating for a moment before he gave up the doll and spun around to follow Rieka and Drusilla into the night.

As the trio vanished into the shadows, the demon with a face full of spines finally produced a curved dagger and sliced his own necktie in half, gasping for air as the knot finally loosened. The two demons fell apart, both tugging the ruined ties away from their respective throats.

"Should we try to find them?" rasped Durian Face.

Sisseroth glared into the shadows and threw the remains of his tie into the dirt. "Don't bother. They'll show themselves again eventually," he croaked. "They lost their haul, anyway." He held the baby doll up in the lamplight.

"I thought that place was all fakes and reproductions."

"It is, mostly," hissed Sisseroth. "But those blood rats went to a lot of trouble to get this. What do you think? Is it authentic? Do that little party trick of yours."

"You want me to show you how my neck is double-jointed?"

"No, you idiot." Sisseroth held out the doll.

"Right." Durian Face closed his eyes and sniffed it. "Definitely mystical. Yeah. There's a consciousness in there. I can smell it. What do you think a couple of vampires wanted a haunted doll for?"

Sisseroth shook his head. "Who knows. We'll give it to Gunnar and let him sort it out."

Across town, Ed's eyelids fluttered and her head lolled listlessly from side to side. "Here we go," she breathed.

CHAPTER FIFTEEN

The sewers were warm and muggy, but even the oppressive fumes couldn't dampen Spike's mood as they made their way back toward Shadwell.

"All right. Got to admit, that could have gone a lot worse," Rieka said.

"It really could have, couldn't it?" agreed Spike. He couldn't stop himself from grinning from ear to ear.

"We should celebrate," suggested Drusilla. "Maybe an orphan or two?" She turned to Rieka. "You can have the bones when we're done."

"So generous." Rieka rolled her eyes.

"Not yet," said Spike. "That was only the first steps of the dance, my sweet. The band's still warming up, and the next bit is the part we've all been rehearsing for."

"Shh." Rieka put a finger to her lips. They were nearing a bend in the tunnel, and she was suddenly tense. If she had been in wolf form, her hackles would most certainly have been up.

"What is—" Spike began, and then a familiar figure came around the corner ahead of them. "Darla?"

"Grandmother!" called Drusilla happily.

"Drusilla," said Darla. "Spike? I've barely seen you in days. Where are the two of you—" Her eyes bounced from Spike to Rieka, and then they narrowed. "Where are the *three* of you headed?"

"Just out having a bit of fun," Spike cut in.

"You know we're not supposed to be picking up meals in the city," Darla chided, still eying Rieka.

"I know." Drusilla sighed. "Spike won't even split an orphan with me."

"It's not like that," said Spike, jabbing a finger at Rieka. "If this one were a meal, she'd have gone bad already. Werewolf."

Darla's eyebrows rose. "I see. And you are keeping a low profile, like Lord Ruthven insisted?" she pressed. "Not stirring up trouble or getting Drusilla involved in any weird nonsense?"

"No," Spike said. "Nope. Definitely not. We're not up to anything weird. Just, you know . . . kinky sex stuff."

Rieka pursed her lips but kept her mouth shut.

"With a werewolf?" asked Darla.

"You know Dru and I are game for anything once." Spike shrugged.

Drusilla nodded. "It's true."

"Full moon in a few days," Spike added with a waggle of his eyebrows.

Beside him, Rieka's expression tightened, but she remained tactfully silent.

Darla shook her head. "Well, I'm glad you've found something to keep yourselves entertained." She relaxed a little. "I'd be lying if

I said I hadn't given it a try myself once. Every vampire needs to be young and reckless for a few decades, I suppose."

"Care to join us?" Drusilla offered.

"Thank you, no," Darla replied. "Not this time. But you enjoy yourselves."

They parted ways, and once the sound of Darla's footsteps was well behind them, Rieka finally broke the silence. "Quick thinking," she conceded. "To be clear, though: It is *never* happening."

"Never say never," said Drusilla.

"Definitely never."

"We'll call it a *maybe*," said Spike.

Rieka glared at them both. "Could we please get back to Hammond's before I murder you myself?"

Darla glanced behind her as she neared the ladder to the surface. Spike and Drusilla had not seemed inclined to follow. That was good. Let them amuse themselves with their newfound stray, so long as they were keeping out of trouble.

She climbed to the surface, not far from Trafalgar Square. Peeking over the rooftops behind her in the moonlight, she could see the smug face of Admiral Nelson atop his towering, ostentatious plinth. She never could understand why men like Nelson were elevated as heroes. He had killed a lot of people and then died. So what? Darla had done the same thing, albeit in reverse order. Where was her statue?

She wound her way toward the gardens that bordered the Thames. Ahead, a man in a dark frock coat and a big, bushy gray beard was trying embarrassingly hard to look as if he wasn't hiding in the shadows of the trees on the Victoria Embankment in the middle of the night. Darla sidled up next to him silently. She didn't say anything at first, just breathed in the sweet smell of the grasses and greenery. Even this close to the river, the gardens were a literal breath of fresh air. London was a town whose smells were built atop the ruins of older smells. The city had found it necessary to install unsightly urinals in the middle of public thoroughfares in a futile attempt to try to convince its citizens to stop peeing wherever they pleased. Compared to the rotting basement, these gardens were idyllic.

The man cleared his throat, looking nervously to the left and right. "Well," he said, "I'm here."

"Good evening, Prime Minister," said Darla. "Or do you still prefer Marquess of Salisbury? You do make it difficult to keep track. It was just viscount the last time we met."

"Call me whatever you like, so long as it isn't *dinner*," replied Salisbury. "Lord above. You don't look as·if you've aged a day," he noted. "Not that you would, I suppose. I certainly have."

It was true. Salisbury had never been a slight man, but he had bulged and sagged over the years like a poorly stuffed sofa. His beard, which had once been coal black, now made him look like a sober Father Christmas.

"I take it you found the note I left," said Darla. "That's good. I went to some trouble to deliver it. You're not an easy man to get close to."

"You didn't." Salisbury huffed. "You delivered the thing to my ruddy nephew. Caused quite the fuss, too."

Darla blinked. "What? No. You're the prime minister. I checked. I may not keep up with every little detail of your monotonous human politics, but prime ministers still live at Number Ten Downing Street, don't they?"

"Not this one." Salisbury shook his head. "Gave those cramped old quarters to Arthur. You baffled the dickens out of the fellow, you should know. You're lucky he brought the note to me in the morning to see if I could make heads or tails of it. I told him it was a cheeky prank and not to think anything of it."

Darla's eye twitched. She was definitely not letting Spike know about this.

"Well. I appreciate you meeting with me on such short notice all the same," said Darla.

"You made it quite clear in your note that it would be injurious to my health if I did not," grumbled Salisbury. "Not that I've much to lose these days. Georgina passed over a year ago."

"My condolences," said Darla. "I liked her. She was sharp."

Salisbury nodded somberly. "It comes for us all." His eyes darted back to Darla. "It comes a lot *faster* for us humans, obviously, but still. Speaking of which, I'm informed that you left five Blackhearth boys with their hearts still beating in their chests the other night."

"Consider it a token of my goodwill."

"Left one of them with a broken collarbone and several fractured ribs."

"Consider it a token of my *moderate* goodwill," she said.

"Well?" Salisbury finally turned to face her properly. "Out with it, then. What is this all about?"

"I would like to come to a more tolerable arrangement between our two communities," answered Darla. "Yes, your people occasionally turn ours to ashes, and ours occasionally rip the throats out of yours and leave their corpses in the gutters—but that's no reason that our two governing bodies cannot be civil."

Salisbury's eyes narrowed. "What is it you want, exactly?"

"An armistice with Blackhearth. Through the end of next month, at least. Oh, and the release of Count Orlok would be nice, if he hasn't been dusted already."

"What happens next month?"

"Darkmarket. Our kind convene to hold occult auctions and trade certain esoteric objects. There is a moratorium on killing locally while the market is in session, so you needn't worry about your citizens' lives. Probably safer in London during the market than any other time, honestly, particularly in the area of Camden Town. Ensuring that it is protected would be a strong step toward building trust and establishing a more lasting arrangement."

"Hmph," Salisbury grunted. "I don't believe in forging permanent alliances, my dear Darla, nor in making lasting enemies. Splendid isolation is the strength of the empire. We float lazily downstream, putting out the occasional diplomatic boat hook to avoid collisions—we do not lash ourselves to the crocodiles sharing the river beside us."

"Blackhearth seems to follow a different philosophy," Darla replied. "That chap with the broken collarbone was quite vocal about their intentions for our kind. Their boat *is* making waves, Prime Minister, and if they continue to escalate hostilities, then they are on their way to making some *very* lasting enemies for the Crown."

"Mm." Salisbury put his thumbs in the pockets of his waistcoat and looked out toward the Thames. When he spoke, his voice was a gruff whisper. "I am not officially aware of Blackhearth, dear lady, just as I am not officially aware of *you*. But, for the sake of argument, let us imagine that the royal family has indeed ordered their clandestine paranormal service to take the offensive against certain supernatural neighbors. In this purely hypothetical scenario, Blackhearth could *not* be considered the aggressors. To be clear, they are only responding defensively to an exponential rise in occult attacks on innocent citizens. Quite frankly, if someone in my position *were* officially aware of such events, then that someone might be obligated to declare an all-out war."

"But that's not *us* doing all that, though," said Darla. "That would be the demon syndicate. Vampires are lying even lower than usual right now. If you have a problem with the demons, take it up with them."

"The general public might find it difficult to tell the difference." Salisbury sighed. "Didn't you tell me once that your own bloodline traced back to a demon?"

Darla bristled. "That's not the point. Having some of the same blood doesn't make you the same. Kings and queens all over Europe are all basically cousins—that hasn't stopped them from going to war with one another at the drop of a hat."

Salisbury conceded the point with a bob of his head. "All right. So the empire's present problem is demons, not vampires—and *your* problem is that Blackhearth is threatening your Noxious Objects Auction—or whatever it's called?"

"Darkmarket."

"Right. It seems to me that you solve one problem by solving the other. If you can curtail this rash of demonic crimes, then I'm sure Edward could be persuaded to order Blackhearth to give Camden a wide berth for the duration of your gruesome gathering."

"I don't control the demons," said Darla.

"It seems nobody does," said Salisbury. "And that is the issue, precisely."

"Fine," Darla grunted. She could feel a pressure headache building behind her eye. "I'll put out my own *diplomatic boat hook* and see what I can do. What about releasing Count Orlok?"

"I don't believe we have him," said Salisbury. "*Officially* or otherwise. But I will make a few inquiries."

Darla nodded and left the prime minister hiding in the shadows of the garden.

She was beginning to feel cautiously optimistic about the whole scheme, but it was like balancing a house of cards. With the Vampires' Guild and Blackhearth tentatively in place, Drusilla had a real shot at a stable future. All that remained was to locate Gunnar, the Hastam demon and Dread Lord of London Town, and convince him to play along. Demons could be reasonable when they wanted to be.

Darla slipped into the underground at Charing Cross. She was all the more pleased that Spike and Drusilla had found a new diversion with which to entertain themselves instead of going after that stupid relic. The last thing she needed was a wild card to bring everything tumbling down.

CHAPTER SIXTEEN

Spike was definitely going to get that relic. The air in Shadwell felt electric as he emerged once more into the night, Drusilla and Rieka close behind him. The gears were already in motion. By the time they made their way back to the Lang Building, Mucker was pacing impatiently. Hammond took his feet off one of the workbenches and sat up straight as Spike and the others entered the old factory, and Ed remained slumped in her chair.

"Well?" Mucker snarled. "What took you tossers so long?"

Drusilla cocked her head at him and smiled pleasantly. "You're going to look me in the eyes when you die," she crooned.

"Promises, promises," Mucker grumbled. "You shoulda been back ages ago. Did anything go wrong?"

"Smooth as a hot knife through a butler," Spike answered.

"It's *butter*," said Rieka.

"I like it my way."

Rieka filled in the crew with the details of the staged heist, the encounter with the demon duo, and their daring escape.

"Excellent." Hammond rubbed his hands when she was finished.

Mucker shook his head. "I still don't understand why you had to stage a break-in at all if we weren't actually planning on taking anything. You three could have skipped all the theatrics and just hand-delivered that stupid doll to Gunnar in the first place."

Rieka snorted. "If you stop to tell us every time you can't understand something, we'll be at this for years."

"Watch yourself, wolf." Mucker jabbed a dirty finger in her direction.

Spike chuckled.

"Don't you start, pretty boy." Mucker turned on him. "At least the *wolf* served a purpose tonight. Care to enlighten the group as to why on Baphomet's black earth you decided to pick a fight with Gunnar's guards and then tried to steal *back* the doll you wanted them to take in the first place?"

"For the same reason the Greeks didn't just *tell* the Trojans the wooden horse was for them, you nit."

"What?" Mucker scowled "Your plan has a horse in it now?"

Spike rubbed his temple. "Unholy hell. Read a book, man."

"Shut up, the lot of you," Hammond barked. "She's talking."

Ed's chest rose as she drew a deep breath. "I think we've arrived," she murmured sleepily.

"Attagirl," said Spike. "What are you seeing?"

"I'm being taken inside Gunnar's building," she said. "Somebody has been sent to announce us. Now we're waiting in the front hall. Oh. Ugh."

"What? What is it?" Hammond asked.

"It's Azerom."

"Who?" said Spike.

"He's a chaos demon. We used to date. This would be so awkward if I wasn't recorporealized in a new vessel right now. I hope he doesn't recognize me. How did the doll look when you left it? Did its hair get all flattened down being stuffed in that satchel for so long?"

"Just let us know when Gunnar arrives," said Spike.

"Oh dear!" Ed gasped.

"What is it?" Hammond demanded.

"Azerom's caught his antlers on the chandelier. He's getting slime all over the crystal. He always was so clumsy with those things. Okay. It's fine. He's out now."

Spike rolled his eyes. "Oh, good."

"Wait," Ed whispered. "I see Gunnar. He looks annoyed. Or maybe . . . amused? It's hard to tell from this angle."

"Pretty sure that's just his face," said Spike.

"He's taken the doll," Ed said. "It worked! He's going to put me in his collection! Oof. That's disorienting. Who carries a baby upside down by the foot? Rude."

"You ate a whole baby only last month," Rieka said.

"Yes, but I held it right side up until I did," Ed replied. "All right. I think we're heading toward the door. Yes. I see the lock."

"You're up." Hammond nodded to Mucker. Mucker licked his lips and produced a pad of paper from his back pocket. He planted himself on a workbench with a stubby pencil hovering over the page.

"Everything is the wrong way up, but I can see the glyphs on the combination," Ed said. "The first one is . . . *shamad*."

Mucker jotted the symbol in his book. "Shamad, that's *annihilation*," he mumbled.

"Next is . . . *mavet*."

The pencil scribbled. "*Death*. Nice."

"It's going around again," Ed whispered. "The third is . . . yes, it's *sheol*. Wait. Shoot!" Ed's brow furrowed ever so slightly.

"What is it?"

"He's shifted his grip. I can't see the lock anymore. I can hardly see anything—he's got a hand covering half my face. Why would anyone hold a doll like this? Honestly."

Spike cursed under his breath.

"Can you try to look . . . harder?" Mucker suggested.

Ed ignored him. "I'm pointed at a blank wall. I have no idea what the fourth symbol is. I can hear him turning it again. I'm missing the fifth, too."

"So glad we went to all this effort for nothing," moaned Rieka.

"That's done it," Ed whispered. "Pretty sure he stopped after the fifth glyph, and I can hear the hinges creaking. The door is opening—oh, *now* he points me forward again."

Mucker glared at the three symbols he had copied over and then added two empty boxes beneath them with big, thick question marks inside. He scratched his stubble.

"He's carrying me up the stairs now," Ed continued. "Hey—take a little care, you big orangutan! I'm a limited edition! It's a good thing they made sturdy dolls in that factory of yours, because Gunnar has no respect for the finer things."

"Priorities, love," Spike urged. "Can you see any cell doors? They should be set into the walls on each landing."

Ed concentrated. "Yes. Hard to see into the windows, though. Looks like there's somebody with wings in that one. The next one looks empty."

"Keep looking," urged Rieka.

"We're going up more stairs," Ed narrated. "Okay. Can't see anything through that one. Yikes, that guy does not look happy to be in there."

"Ermack?" Rieka asked. Her whole body looked tense.

"Not unless he's grown a set of tusks since he got nabbed," Ed answered. "I'm going up one more flight. Looks like we're on the top floor. I still haven't seen—hold on."

"What?" Hammond was leaning in.

"Is that . . . ? Yes! It's him! Ermack put his face up to the window as Gunnar and I passed. He's in the second cell on the highest level."

Rieka slapped the table beside her so hard a cloud of dust billowed off of it. "I knew he was still alive." She drew an uneven breath and let it out in a puff.

Hammond gave her a pat on the shoulder. "Told ya we'd get the old boy back."

"We haven't got anyone back yet," said Spike. "Hush up, now. Your demonic dearest is only the first half of the job. You still there, Ed?"

"I'm heading through a door at the landing," Ed answered. "Gunnar's dropped me in some sort of a storage room." She let out a sudden gasp. "Lords below, he's got a lot of goodies up here. We could retire for centuries on a handful of this loot."

"I don't suppose you can see a pinkie finger somewhere in the mix?" Spike asked. "Old? Finger-size?"

"You can come and look for it yourself, thank you," said Ed. "And do not forget to pick up my doll. I would much rather snap back to myself sooner rather than later—I do *not* fancy being stuck outside my body when Gunnar finds out his latest trophy has been stolen right out of his tower. Also, did you see the detail work on my tiny dress? The lace is just darling. This might be my favorite vessel yet."

"We'll get you out of there." Hammond patted her limp shoulder. "Nice work, Ed. Now we know where the bastard's keeping our boy."

"Great," said Spike. "If Mucker does his bit on the lock, then it should be a straight shot up the stairs to spring your demon, a quick game of find-the-finger and snag-the-dolly, and we're out and gone under the cover of supernatural silence before Gunnar knows we were ever there."

"I only wish we had got a few more of those glyphs." Hammond turned to Mucker. "What do you think? Do we need to find another way in?"

Mucker blew a bit of broken pencil lead off of his paper. "No. It's fine. I can work with three outta five. I'll just need a solid minute to sort out the other two once we're inside."

Hammond's shoulders relaxed, and he nodded with visible relief.

"We still need to buy him that minute," said Spike. "How much scratch were you able to pull together?"

"Nearly four hundred sterling," said Hammond, patting a leather valise on the chair beside him. "Had to cash in some valuable favors to get it all."

"And you're willing to bet the whole purse on black? Last chance to call the whole thing off, mate. I'm not great at math, but four hundred sterling split between six people is a pretty decent consolation prize."

"Six." Drusilla giggled. "Six, six, six . . ."

"Nobody's backing out," Rieka said. "We found him. We're getting him."

Hammond nodded. "Nobody gets left."

"Good," said Spike. "That's what I want to hear. Time to make those coins jingle."

CHAPTER SEVENTEEN

Wych Street wore a thick shroud of fog, the haze wrapping itself around corners and rolling lazily down the cobblestones. Even if the gargoyles atop Gunnar's mansion had been surveying the area, they would have been hard-pressed to see a thing. If they had been listening, they might have heard the faint scrape of metal grating on nearby flagstones—but the sound, too, was largely swallowed by the fog. It was a perfect night for finding oneself up to no good.

Across the street, Spike held Drusilla's hand as she stepped up out of the sewer into the cool night air.

Hammond slid the grate carefully back into place behind them. "That's all of us," he whispered. "You all set over there?"

"We're good," Mucker's voice grunted from the cabin of a black carriage. He clambered out and dropped to the ground, dusting off his hands on the sides of a shabby brown jacket. He still wore the derby, which looked—if possible—even rattier than it had a week ago.

Rieka poked her head inside the carriage. "Hey, Ed," she whispered. "Be a doll and hang on to this for me until we get back, won't you?" She tossed a light bundle onto Ed's lap.

Ed's arms remained loose by her sides, her eyelids shut. "Hilarious," she grumbled. "I have no idea what's happening. Where exactly are you leaving my body again? I would be much more comfortable knowing I was safe in the Lang Building."

"You're fine," Hammond assured her in hushed tones. "We've tucked you into a broken-down carriage—out of the way and out of sight, but still easy for us to get to you in a pinch if necessary. There's an Inn of Chancery across the street from Gunnar's, and you're parked in a sort of carriage house beside it. There's even sewer access right under our feet for a quick getaway when it's all over."

"Ugh." Ed's nose crinkled. "I am not mucking through the sewers like a common rat. I'll have you know this dress came from Paris."

"That dress came from a dead tourist," Rieka said.

"A dead *French* tourist," Ed countered.

"Don't be such a porcelain princess," Mucker piped in. "It's just a sewer. How do you think we got you here in the first place?"

"No." Ed gasped. "You didn't."

"We sure did," added Rieka. "And we might have let your head scrape the wall a few times by accident, so if you notice any gunk up there later, that's probably why."

Ed let out a horrified, whimpering squeak.

"Enough," said Hammond. "They're only takin' the piss, Ed." Beside him, Mucker shook his head. Hammond cleared his throat. "You can get home however you like once the job is done. Until then, just sit tight."

"Not as though I have a lot of choice in the matter, do I?" Ed sighed. "Oh—one more thing. Could you please tell them to fetch my doll *before* doing any brutal mutilations? And make sure I have a clear view of the show if they do. It's been too long since I've had a nice viewing."

"We'll be sure to tack your personal entertainment onto our priorities list while we're trying not to get ourselves dusted," Spike muttered. He surveyed the group one more time. "Okay, team. This is it. You all know your roles. Let's go be bad guys."

"And bad women," added Rieka.

"Sure," said Spike. "Also bad women."

"Technically *they're* bad guys, too," said Mucker, nodding toward Gunnar's place. "Wait. Does that make us the *good* guys?"

Spike bristled as if he had tasted something rancid. "What? No. We're not the *good* guys. Do we look like *good* guys? We're the *worse* guys—the thoroughly awful guys who are so bad we make *other* bad guys look . . . stupid. And also bad women."

"Thank you," said Rieka with a curt nod.

"Fine speech," said Hammond. "All right, Rieka. You and I are up first."

The two of them stepped together through the fog toward the towering mansion.

"Feeling confident?" Rieka whispered.

Hammond jiggled the leather valise clutched in his fist. "I can sell it," he said, forcing an unconvincing smile and a wink. "Trust me."

Spike, Drusilla, and Mucker kept to the shadows as they moved into position. Across the street, they could hear Hammond's fist rap on the front door.

They waited.

"Mm. The rain feels nice," Drusilla said softly.

Spike and Mucker exchanged a glance. Spike cleared his throat. "It's not raining, love."

"Of course it is," she said. "But it's all on the inside—for now."

"I don't know why you insisted on bringing her," Mucker whispered, shaking his head. "She is a liability, and you know it."

"I know that you're an absolute sodding turnip," Spike whispered back, "but we brought you."

"Are you sure she'll even be able to cross the threshold?" Mucker growled. "She should stay here with Ed."

"Am I not coming to the party?" Drusilla's eyes seemed to find their way back from some distant land. "But I got all dressed up."

"Of course you're coming." Spike cupped her cheek in his hand. "You know dancing over the corpses of our enemies isn't any fun if you're not there to dance with me." He shot Mucker an acid glare. "And she'll be able to cross the threshold. Mr. Gunnar himself extended a personal invitation for her to join me the next time I came calling." He turned back to Drusilla. "It would be rude of you not to."

Drusilla smiled. "Wouldn't want to be rude."

Mucker ground his teeth but didn't press the matter.

Across the street, the demon Cricklewood had opened the door and was speaking in clipped tones to Hammond and Rieka. The rhythm of Hammond's deep baritone carried across the street in reply, leaving the details of his words behind in the fog.

Drusilla's hand wrapped itself around Spike's arm while they waited. "It's a lovely gift," she whispered.

He put a hand on hers. "And it's almost yours, my dear."

She gave his arm a squeeze. "It's already mine, silly," she said.

Spike's brow furrowed. "It *will* be. It's just that it's still stuck in Gunnar's treasure room, remember?"

"No it's not." Drusilla leaned her head on his shoulder. "It's right here. It's happening."

Spike felt a tingle run up his spine and ripple out to his ears.

"I'm sure you two mushy monsters love each other to the bottoms of your cold, un-beating hearts and all that," Mucker mumbled. "But do you think you can keep yer clothes on long enough to do the job we came for? Because we're up."

Spike turned his attention back in time to see the door to Gunnar's mansion click shut. The three of them hurried silently across the cobblestones and dove into a pool of darkness beside the front steps. They could hear the murmur of voices from within. Phase two had begun.

Rieka's senses were flooded as she followed Hammond into the mansion. Her head swam with clashing scents. The smoky odor of the fireplace was strongest, but it did not cover up a distinct soapy, coppery stink saturating all the carpets and drapes. Somebody had cleaned a lot of blood out of this house. A lot. Rieka had to admit they had done a decent job. She was only too aware of how persistent bloodstains could be. She was also keenly aware that she didn't want them to be cleaning *hers* out of the carpet next.

"Master Gunnar will see you soon," Cricklewood informed them. "You may await his arrival in the drawing room." The two of them followed the demon doorman as he led them into a warmly lit space to the left of the foyer, the smell of cedarwood and tobacco heavy in the air. There were leather armchairs on one side of a low table, and on the other sat a wide sofa adorned with intricate carvings of grotesque beasts putting human figures through all manner of torture. A broad stained-glass window took up one wall, mostly comprised of varying shades of glittering red—none of the nine levels of hell were known for cool colors—although there were a few splashes of a very pleasant emerald in the eighth circle, where several glass serpents were coiling themselves around some unhappy-looking glass thieves. On the whole, it was a lovely composition. Set into the opposite wall was a broad hearth, a fire crackling away within it.

"Not bad," Hammond mumbled to Rieka under his breath. "If we're going to be fed to the hellhounds, at least we get to feel a bit swanky first."

He took a seat on the sofa, holding the valise in his lap and drumming his fingers on the handle. Rieka sat next to him. From her position, she had a clear view of the foyer. A pair of demon guards stood in front of the staircase, eyes on the front door, right where Spike had said they would be. The guards would have to go. This plan needed to work, or the whole thing would be a bust.

"Humans are not typically permitted on the furniture," Cricklewood said dryly. She looked up at him, but he did not make eye contact. "If you would like," he continued, pointedly addressing Hammond, "I could have her brought down to the kitchens and bled for you? It is a service our staff is only too happy to provide while you wait."

Rieka's eyes widened. "Excuse me?"

"Much appreciated," Hammond answered. "But not this time. Don't worry. Not technically human, this one." He gave the demon doorman a wink. "It's all right. We're all monsters here."

"My mistake." Cricklewood gave Rieka an unapologetic glance and turned to go.

"I would really enjoy killing that one," Rieka whispered.

"Stick to the plan," Hammond murmured.

They did not have to wait long before a deep voice boomed from the door on the opposite end of the room, "You've got guts, Harry Hammond. I'll give you that." Gunnar strode into the room, followed by two of his underlings. "Can't promise you'll still have them by the time we're done here. But you've got them."

Gunnar might not have been quite the mountain of a man that Hammond was, but of the two, the barrel-chested, broad shouldered demon certainly looked like a more polished draft. He wore an immaculately tailored shirt and his crown of horns was freshly buffed. The firelight played along the bright red of his brawny arms—each of them as wide as Rieka's entire body.

The minions who entered behind him were no giants, but they still looked plenty deadly. The one on Gunnar's right was a copper-skinned Fyarl, his suit specially tailored to leave room for his jagged shoulder ridges. He had very traditional horns that curled over the sides of his head like a ram's, and a pair of curved daggers that hung from his belt. On Gunnar's left stood a vengeance demon, her dress the same charcoal gray as the Fyarl's suit. The slender ribbon around her neck was bloodred, maintaining the syndicate color scheme. She wore her natural face, a decaying network of ruddy blisters that looked less like skin and more like a topographical map of a battle zone. Rieka respected the natural look. It might have been nauseating, but at least it was honest. She liked to know who she was dealing with.

Gunnar took a deep breath before he spoke. "Got to admit," he said at last, "I'm a little disappointed, Harry. You rolling over and turning yourself in like this—it takes all the fun out of tracking you down."

"Nobody's rolling over just yet," said Hammond.

"No?" Gunnar chuckled and shook his head. "London isn't yours anymore, vampire. I've given you plenty of chances to get that through your thick skull. Say, how big do you think that skull of yours is, by the way? Your lady friend's here doesn't look like more than a coffee mug, but I think I might be able to get a decent soup bowl out of yours."

"We're not here to fight," Hammond said. "In fact, we're here to bargain."

Gunnar rolled his eyes. "That's cute. Look, I'm sure you've got a great offer and *blah-blah-blah, please don't kill me*—but I'm a busy guy. Accounts to settle. People to eviscerate."

"I'll get right to it, then." Hammond set the bag on the table between them. "The Bloody Tower job," he said. "We must've cost your crew around, what, two hundred pounds?" He clicked open the valise. Gunnar raised an eyebrow. "This is near twice that."

"I'm listening." Gunnar eyed the bag before dropping himself into the armchair across from the two of them. "Although I seem to recall one of my favorite demons getting vaporized as a result of that particular incident. Holy-water bath is a nasty way to go. Hey, Cricklewood!" he called over his shoulder. "What was that guy's name? The ugly one?"

"Hoburth, sir," Cricklewood replied.

"His name was Hoburth," said Gunnar meaningfully.

"I'm sure he'll be missed." Hammond nodded. "Your team dusted two of ours, too, so I think the ledgers balance out there.

The thing is, you've got another one of ours upstairs. A demon. He's called Ears. I want to trade for him."

"No," said Gunnar.

"You didn't let me finish," said Hammond.

"You were finished before you started," Gunnar said. "You thought you could come into my home and just name your own price for one of my trophies? What is it with you bloodsuckers? Every time I let one of you parasites into my home, you're trying to leave with a party favor. I already told that slayer-killer friend of yours, I don't give up what's mine. What you've got in that bag is barely enough to buy you and your lady friend safe passage out my front door—and even that generous offer is rapidly expiring."

"I wasn't talking about the money," said Hammond. "Look. You and I both know Ears is not your finest catch. The guy can't even throw a respectable punch—weak wrists. What if I could offer you a real scrapper to take his place? Someone who's warmed their fangs in more necks than I can count? A prize more worthy of your trophy case?"

Gunnar made a modest effort to conceal his interest. "What sort of trophy did you have in mind?"

Hammond swallowed. Rieka caught his eye as it darted to her and back to Gunnar. *Come on*, she urged with her eyes. *No hesitation now.*

"How about . . . a *werewolf*?" Hammond said.

Rieka froze for just a moment as she processed Hammond's words. Her brows rose on her forehead, and her nostrils flared. "*What?*"

CHAPTER EIGHTEEN

Rieka stood bolt upright. "That was not the plan!" she hissed. "You were supposed to offer him that cocky bloodsucker. What the hell are you doing?"

Hammond kept his eyes on Gunnar. "Well?" he said.

Gunnar let out a deep belly laugh. "You think I'm about to trade a third-level Kakophonos demon for your mangy guard dog?"

"I wouldn't underestimate her," Hammond insisted.

Rieka's jaw hung open at the betrayal she was witnessing.

"She's embraced the wolf," Hammond continued. "It's always there. Just under the surface."

Gunnar shook his head, still grinning in amusement. "I respect the gambit, and I did enjoy watching you double-cross a trusted ally right to her face. That was exquisite. I'll treasure that. Really. But I'm not giving back Ermack. Got plans for him already. That demon's got real power. Should've seen him when we brought him in. My left ear was ringing for a week after, the cheeky bastard. But now he's mine, and I do not part with what's mine." He licked his sharp teeth and regarded the two of them for a moment. "You can go, Hammond. I will, however, keep the werewolf. She looks as if she's well done with you, anyway."

Rieka's throat tightened. "Not happening," she said, hoping she sounded more confident than she felt.

"I wasn't asking you, sweetheart." Gunnar gave a lazy nod, and the demons on his left and right advanced toward Rieka.

"Thanks a lot, boss," she spat.

"Nothing personal," Hammond mumbled.

In a flash, Rieka's studded truncheon was in her hand and she had bent into a crouch, muscles tensed for combat.

The demon guards closed in.

Rieka growled. A solid kick with her boot sent the low table spinning into the vengeance demon, who caught it hard in the stomach and tumbled backward, pound notes and coins spraying across the floor as the valise went flying. Not taking a moment to survey the damage, Rieka whirled and clocked the Fyarl as hard as she could with the truncheon. Her hand stung from the impact, and she nearly dropped the weapon, but the demon barely flinched.

"Hey." The Fyarl rubbed his chin. "That hurt."

Rieka gulped.

There was a clatter behind her, and a moment later, the vengeance demon grabbed her from behind, pinning her arms to her sides. The Fyarl smirked. "My turn," he said, and he drew one of the curved daggers from his belt.

The arms around her were too tight for Rieka to push her way out of them, so she threw her shoulders back into her captor instead. At the same moment, she jolted forward, running right up the legs of the Fyarl until she could kick herself into a backflip off his face. It was enough to rattle the Fyarl's balance, sending him stumbling backward. Rieka let the momentum propel her over her captor's shoulders, breaking the demon's grip. She regained her footing as quickly as she could, slipping back into a low fighting stance as the demons rallied.

Two more demons had appeared, helping lift the Fyarl back to his feet. These must be the guards from the staircase, come to join the fight. Great. Because two against one wasn't already unfair? Cricklewood had also slipped behind Gunnar's chair, his eyes on Rieka. "Would you like me to summon additional personnel, sir?" he asked.

"That won't be necessary." Gunnar waved him away.

"Don't be so sure of yourself," Rieka panted. Four demons now formed a half circle around her, closing in slowly. "I've had worse odds."

"Cute." Gunnar smirked. "Try not to scuff the mahogany."

Spike tentatively peeked through the first-floor window. "Let's go," he whispered.

Mucker was already at the door, lock-picks at the ready, but the knob clicked open in his hand without resistance. With agonizing care, he pulled the door open wide enough to peek inside.

The foyer was empty, and the sounds of a violent fight coming from the next room were enough to shake the walls. Mucker motioned, and Spike and Drusilla slid inside as silently as a pair of moths on a breeze.

Spike glanced to his left as they swept across the lobby floor, and for the briefest of instants, he locked eyes with Rieka. She had her back to the far wall, facing off against four demons at once, already surrounded by broken furniture. Her attackers' attention was too fixed on Rieka for any of them to notice the vampires creeping through the foyer—and in another moment, Rieka turned her focus away from Spike and back to the task at hand. A skinny demon pounced on her, clawlike fingers extended. Spike was halfway up the stairs and out of sight when he heard a loud crack, a thud, and the demon's groan of pain. The wolf could fight, he gave her that, but it would not be long before the demons stopped taking turns.

From the top of the stairs, the hallway provided a clear shot to the vault door. Spike slowed, scanning the area and letting Mucker move ahead of him. The hallway had no convenient alcoves in which to hide and no high ceilings with shadowy rafters on which to perch. There would be no escaping into the safety of the sewers this time. If anyone approached, the team would be completely exposed until Mucker got that lock open.

Spike came to a stop behind Mucker, catching Drusilla's eye as she drew up beside him. Her face was aglow with the thrill of the crime, and Spike could tell without asking that she would be all too giddy if they *were* spotted and needed to fight their way out. He also knew that their chances of surviving against the full force of Gunnar's entire crew were less than positive.

Mucker knelt in front of the lock and got to work. "*Shamad*," he mumbled, making an elaborate gesture over the mechanism before turning the central wheel. "*Mavet . . . Sheol*."

There was another loud thump and a crash like a vase shattering, and then the foyer fell unsettlingly quiet.

"Got a feeling we're gonna want to be on the other side of that door real soon, mate," Spike whispered.

"How about you don't tell me how to open locks, and I won't tell you how to be a useless boot heel," Mucker hissed back. "Ed only gave me three outta five. Let's see. *Shedim . . . Dahm?*" Mucker stopped, taking his hands off the lock slowly. Five glyphs glowed faintly on the wheel. He straightened and gave the door a tug. It didn't budge. He cursed at the mechanism and knelt again. "Okay. From the top: *Shamad . . .*"

Spike sighed and cracked his neck. "Well, Dru," he whispered. "There are worse ways to go out than fighting an army of demons side by side with you."

Drusilla shook her head. "This isn't it," she said matter-of-factly. "We've got loads to do yet. We're going to visit Italy. And Prague. And California. We're going to meet so many people"— she sighed wistfully—"and kill as many of them as we can."

"That's right, princess." Spike smiled at her, trying to keep his expression optimistic. "Bodies to the sky."

In the drawing room, Rieka was breathing hard. The pair of demon guards from the stairwell were now holding her by her wrists, their grips like steel. The vengeance demon had a bloody lip, and the Fyarl had chipped a horn—but her small victories only seemed to have made them angrier. She struggled uselessly against their hold.

From his comfortable chair, Gunnar clicked his tongue. "That vase you just broke was from the Ming dynasty," he chided. "Had a really nice likeness of an old friend of mine on it. Also the ashes of that old friend inside it. What was her name, Cricklewood?"

"Pipa Jing," Cricklewood said.

"That's the one. Pipa Jing," Gunnar agreed. He took a deep breath. "Okay, look. This was amusing at first, but I think it's time—" He stopped midsentence. His eyes narrowed, and he cocked his head toward the foyer. His nose crinkled, and he sniffed.

Rieka's heart thudded in her chest.

Reflected firelight danced on the Hastam's polished horns.

Gunnar stood up, slowly. "Cricklewood," he said. "Were we expecting any other visitors tonight?"

"*Shamad . . . Mavet . . . Sheol . . . Shedim . . . Karath?*" Mucker muttered. Again, the glyphs glowed around the wheel. Again, the door refused to budge. "Bloody hell. I swear, I've got all but that fifth glyph sorted."

"You have no idea what you're doing, do you?" Spike hissed.

Mucker ignored him, beginning the sequence over again.

Spike watched the stairs. He could hear the squeak of a chair sliding back, and the thud of heavy footsteps nearing.

"We're about to have company," he whispered.

But then there was another noise.

It began like a ripping, shredding sound, melting gradually into an animal snarl, followed by yelps of surprise from a couple of demons downstairs.

Finally, Hammond's deep voice echoed up from the drawing room. "I warned you," he said, "she keeps the wolf close to the surface."

CHAPTER NINETEEN

I t was still two days until the full moon. The wolf would have been more powerful if she had waited, but Rieka would have also had a harder time remembering who she was in the heat of the moment.

Thoughts came to Rieka differently in wolf form. They were leaner. Sharper.

A demon reached for the scruff of her neck, and she whipped her head to the side instinctively, her jaw snapping shut. The demon's hide was like the hard scales of a serpent—tough, but almost brittle under the pressure of her bite. The flesh below was less resilient. The human part of Rieka couldn't help but recall the texture of a fresh baguette. The crackle of the exterior and then the warmth of the steaming-soft bread within. The thought brought back happy memories.

The demon, not enjoying the same peaceful sensory association, let out a scream of pain.

Rieka tightened her grip and wrenched her head to the side.

With a gush of heat around her lips and a crunch like fresh celery, the arm dropped to the ground.

Gunnar cursed. "Mind the carpet, you incompetent gnat! Go bleed out in the basement! Baphomet's balls. Will one of you please muzzle that mangy cur!"

The Fyarl came at her next, a curved blade clutched in each hand. Rieka feinted left and then darted to the right. The Fyarl might have been fast enough to catch the misdirection if his feet hadn't skidded in the growing pool his associate was hemorrhaging onto the drawing-room floor. It was all he could do to keep his feet under him as he skated toward the stained-glass window. He nearly had his momentum back under control when a set of heavy paws hammered into his back, and he tumbled face-first through all nine circles of hell, crimson shards and soft metal fixtures exploding all around him. He hit the flagstones below with a wet crack and the tinkling of broken glass.

Rieka landed on the floor in a low crouch, her muscles tight and her hackles raised. Two down, two to go. The remaining demon guards looked to their employer nervously. Gunnar did not appear happy about the window. Rieka's eyes had taken on the full, wild fury of a cornered animal. If there was any humanity behind that gaze, it was buried deep.

"Stand back," Hammond called, finally pushing himself up off of the sofa. "Give her some room. I can usually get through to her when she's in this state."

Gunnar gestured with mock benevolence. "Be my guest."

The vampire took small, slow steps as he eased forward toward the panting werewolf. Rieka's eyes darted left and right, her muscles coiled under the thick fur.

"It's all right," Hammond said gently. "You know me. Remember?"

Rieka's shifting eyes finally locked on Hammond and narrowed. Her furry brow creased and her snout wrinkled as bloody lips pulled back in a sneer to reveal fangs like steak knives.

"Remember?" Hammond croaked again hopefully.

Rieka launched herself at him, sinking her teeth into Hammond's thick shoulder. He howled in pain, and the two of them tumbled over the broken remains of the coffee table.

"I think she remembers." Gunnar chuckled, stepping back to let the two have space to tear at each other.

Hammond swatted Rieka's ears with his free hand, but she did not loosen her grip. He flailed his arms, reaching behind himself, searching frantically for a weapon of any kind—accidentally knocking the brass fire irons out of his reach and then settling for his own open valise. His fingers found the handle, and he pummeled Rieka in the head with the leather bag, coins jingling and papers fluttering around them until she finally unclenched her jaws. Before he even had time to push himself to his feet, her fangs sank into his ankle and he, too, was whipped across the room and out the already-broken window.

Hammond's landing was softened only slightly by the Fyarl, whose head bounced off the sidewalk with a *clack* as Hammond slammed into him from above and rolled onto the paving stones.

Rieka bounded out the window a moment later, snarling and snapping at Hammond's heels as he stumbled and staggered to get away, off into the fog of Wych Street.

In the hallway upstairs, Spike was pacing anxiously, clenching and unclenching his fists. Mucker cursed under his breath and began the sequence for the dozenth time.

Drusilla hummed softly to herself. "Everything's going to be fine, my love," she said.

Spike's face was tense. "*How* is it going to be fine?"

Drusilla considered. "Angel," she said, her voice taking on a singsong cadence.

Spike cringed. "He's not coming, love. We've been over this."

The sounds of glass tinkling had ceased, and Spike could hear the low mumble of Gunnar's voice snarling commands. "I don't care," the Dread Lord of London Town was growling. "Double the guards. Now. Tell Sisseroth and Korvul to get their teams back here, too. That bastard Hammond is up to something more than just making a mess of my house. I can smell it."

Perfect. Spike's jaw clenched. Demonic reinforcements were on the way. At any moment, that doorman and whatever was left of those demon guards would be returning to their posts, and then it would only take one peek up the stairs for Team Vampire to be spotted. Maybe it was better to scrap the whole thing and make a break for it now, before the cavalry arrived.

"*Sheol . . . Shedim . . . Mal'akh,*" Mucker murmured. He flinched at the sound of heavy tumblers clunking into place within the mechanism. He tugged. The door swung open.

All three of them blinked at the open passage.

"And get whoever usually does the carpets over here, too!" barked Gunnar from downstairs. "That rug is Akkadian!"

Mucker spun inside and gestured frantically for the others to hurry. Spike practically shoved Drusilla inside the tower, and Mucker pulled the heavy door closed behind them.

There was silence in the dim corridor.

The three of them waited for several seconds, half expecting the door to whip open again, but the moment came and passed. Spike fumbled for the switch, and then, with a flicker, the gaslights along the walls gradually sputtered to life.

"Knew we could do it," said Spike. "See? We're in. Everything going according to plan. No *angelic* intervention needed."

Drusilla shrugged. "I was right," she said.

"It was not sodding *Angelus*."

"Technically," grunted Mucker, edging past them, "the last glyph I needed was *Mal'akh*. Means *angel*."

Drusilla reached a finger up and tapped Spike on the nose. "See? I told you."

Spike shook his head. "Seriously?"

"She could've ruddy well told *me*," Mucker grumbled. "Would've saved us all some time and tension."

Together, the three of them crept forward and up into the tower stronghold.

Across the street, Hammond massaged his shoulder as he leaned on the wall of the carriage house. "Oof. I'm going to be feeling this all week," he wheezed.

"You're the one who told me to make it look like a convincing attack," Rieka said from inside as she buttoned up the spare overalls she had stashed in a bundle on Ed's lap before the job. The rancid tang of demon blood clung to her gums. She was going to need to gargle with paint thinner to get that taste out of her mouth. Beside her, Ed's head bobbed ever so slightly, her eyes still closed.

"Well, you had *me* convinced for a while there," Hammond grumbled. "You do remember that releasing the wolf was only meant to be a last resort, right?"

"There were too many of them. I didn't see you jumping in to get slashed to ribbons."

Hammond winced as he rotated his shoulder experimentally. "You were doing so well. I was mesmerized." He poked his head through the door. "Ask Ed if she's seen anything yet."

"Nothing yet," Ed breathed from within the carriage. "Still quiet in Gunnar's treasure room."

"It's about to get a lot less quiet," whispered Rieka, peering out the door past Hammond. "I think you should get inside, boss."

Hammond slipped hastily into the carriage house and pulled the door closed behind him as quietly as he could. Together, they crouched at the window to peer outside. A handful of shady figures were emerging from the mist at the end of the street. Demons in prim gray dresses and sharply cut suits poured in from around corners and between buildings, giving the impression that the heavy fog was coalescing into solid forms. Rieka counted twenty-three before she lost track.

"I'm guessing they aren't here for the monthly tiddlywinks tournament," whispered Hammond.

"Maybe they're just arriving as a precaution?" Rieka breathed. "You and I caused an awful row. Think there's any chance the demons don't actually know that our team is on the inside?"

"Hey!" yelled a beady-eyed demon from across the street, waving at one of his comrades up the lane. "Hey, Gnarl! You hear? Yeah, three of them! In the tower! We're gonna murder the snot out of them. Oh, man. I would *not* want to be those guys right now. It's gonna be so violent. I'm really looking forward to the murdering. Hurry up."

Hammond swallowed. "I think they know."

"They're dead." Rieka slumped down to the cold floor, her back against the wall. "Our whole team is dead—if they're lucky—and Ermack is no closer to being free from that damned tower."

"Don't go counting our lot out just yet," grunted Hammond. "They may not look like much, but those vampires up there are some of the sharpest villains in all England. No, really. You haven't seen them in action, not properly. Drusilla's got honest-to-goodness premonitions, and Spike is keen as razor blades. You can bet those two already know the plan is going sideways, and they're two steps ahead of those fool demons. Mark my words."

Several stories above the street, Spike and Drusilla were blissfully unaware.

CHAPTER TWENTY

D o you think they have names?" Drusilla asked, her eyes drifting to the ceiling as they made their way up the stairs of Gunnar's private tower.

Spike glanced around. "Who—the people in all the cells? I'm sure they've got names, Dru. You should see the one he's got in the basement. It's called *Sorm*."

"Not them," Drusilla laughed. "The funny little animals in the ceiling. I think that one's a ferret."

Spike followed her eyes to a snarling stone grotesquerie perched in the woodwork.

"Those are gargoyles, love. Ornamental. They're only meant to look nasty."

"I'm going to call that one Henrietta."

The gargoyle did not object.

"I hate it when villains go in for all this overly dramatic decor," Spike said as they pressed past Henrietta and up the next floor. "Foreboding black spires on the roof, skulls hanging over the breadbox, sacrificial daggers framing the toilet. It's the twentieth century, mate. Just buy some nice brass fixtures and stop trying to impress everybody."

"I dunno." Mucker shrugged. "A polished skull can make a nice accent to any modern abode, I think. I stuck a candle on one at my place. I use it to prop up some books."

"And that's why nobody likes you," Spike said. "Well. One of the many reasons."

Spike jumped as a cell next to him shuddered. Inside, a red-headed brute with a bushy beard and a drab green face threw his shoulder against the door. The etchings in the metal glowed, and the bruiser bounced off it, panting angrily.

"Troll," Mucker said.

"I know what a troll is," Spike huffed, straightening. "Met a handful of the bloody berks in Stockholm. If it weren't for the charm on his cell, he could take that door apart."

"Rotten luck for him, then." Mucker sneered and tapped the glass. "Sorry, mate. We're not rescuing any ugly buggers today. Maybe next time."

The troll growled and flashed him an obscene gesture.

"Come on," Spike prompted. "Tight schedule to keep."

They reached the topmost landing shortly, and Spike hurried over to the second cell. "This is him?" Spike asked, peering through the glass. The demon within the cell was slouching on a low slab. He was hairless with slightly pointed ears and the athletic physique of an insurance consultant. He could pass for an average human, if one overlooked the pale purple skin. "He doesn't look like much."

At the sound of Spike's voice, the demon looked up and scowled suspiciously. "That seems unnecessary," he said, but his expression lightened when Mucker poked his head into view.

"That's our boy, all right," Mucker confirmed. "Okay, Ears, you lavender lummox—let's get you out of here so I can get paid."

"Where's Rieka?" the demon asked, craning his neck to peer through the window.

"With any luck," said Mucker, "she's already wagging her eager tail at the rally point, waiting for us to pop her favorite treat out of lockup. Now hush up. I got a job to do."

A smile spread across the demon's face as Mucker knelt in front of the door and got to work. The vampire spread a leather tool roll out on the ground beside him as he surveyed the etchings. Spike peered over his shoulder. The kit held the usual lock-picks and steel wedges, but also oddly carved bones, scrolls of parchment, and bits of metal that looked like slim branding irons.

"Well?" Mucker glanced over his shoulder. "What are you two dossers hanging around for? This is gonna take a beat. Go make yourselves useful and fetch the fancy dolly."

"How long do you need?" Spike asked.

"As long as it takes. Longer if you keep chattering at me," Mucker said. "This ain't a simple jimmy job. Every one of these cells is bespoke crafted to suppress the specific strengths of whatever poor sod is inside it. High-end arcana, this is. Plus there's a deadbolt."

"So," Spike said, "five minutes?"

Mucker sniffed and shrugged. "Give or take. Now piss off so I can concentrate."

Drusilla was already making her way toward the room at the end of the landing. The door hung ajar—only a fool would be suicidal enough to make it this far, so why should Gunnar bother to lock the thing? One more animalistic gargoyle scowled down from the molding atop the doorframe. It looked vaguely like an angry bug-eyed otter, but an otter that had been carved by an artist who had never actually seen one in the wild, just heard them described in great detail by an elderly neighbor who did not care for otters. Drusilla reached up and patted it affectionately on the snout as she entered.

The storeroom was breathtaking. Gems and gold coins spilled out of squat chests and onto the wide tables that ran along each of the walls of the room. Rings and talismans and goblets littered every available surface, and additional chests had been stuffed unceremoniously atop one another beneath the tables, as if their abundance were a mild inconvenience rather than an absolute bounty. Shelves on the far wall were stacked with leather-bound books and scrolls, a few of them so old the parchment looked as if it might fall apart at the lightest touch. Some artifacts sat in places of honor, resting on prim little pedestals with tidy bronze inscriptions, while others lay upside down and sideways, as if someone had upended a burlap sack full of priceless rarities onto a table.

"So many pretties." Drusilla swept her hand just above the esoteric items as though her fingers were floating on an invisible wave. "That one's a Sobekian Blood Stone," she cooed. "And that's a Band of Blacknill, and an Orb of Ramjarin."

Spike nudged a short onyx statue with his foot. "I found a goat man diddling a mermaid. Is that anything?"

"I can hear something," said Drusilla. She turned her attention to the table on their left.

"Is it a pinkie finger?" asked Spike. "What's a finger sound like?" His eyes scanned the table to their right. A heavy bronze bell sat on a velvet-cushioned plinth with the words JERICHO DOORBELL inscribed on the plaque. He thought about tapping it with a fingernail and then reconsidered.

"Here you are!" Drusilla reached down and scooped something up. When she turned, Spike could see it was a familiar baby doll clad in a frilly pink dress. Drusilla held the doll closer to her ear. "What's that?"

"I'm pretty sure it doesn't work that way, pet," said Spike. "Ed can only listen and watch from this end. She doesn't speak through the doll."

"Maybe not to you," said Drusilla.

Spike opened his mouth but then thought better of it and let the matter drop, turning his attention back to his search.

"Aha!" His eyes spied a glass case no larger than a cigar box lying on its side. It was framed around the corners with ornate metalwork and topped with a fancy, embellished cross. Within the box was a red cloth and—Spike's lips parted in a wide smile— lying directly on the cloth was a dark, shriveled human finger. "Gotcha," he said aloud.

"Spike." Drusilla's voice was edged with concern. "She says something's happening." She held the doll in the crook of her arm like it was a real child.

"I told you, love," Spike said gently. "She can't talk to . . . Hold on." His brow furrowed. "I hear something, too."

As if from far away, the faintest whisper of a voice was speaking. Spike strained his ears, leaning closer to the baby doll.

"I just do what the boss says," the voice murmured. Soft footsteps followed.

Spike's head shot toward the door. "Sodding hell, Dru," he whispered. "That's not coming from the doll. It's coming from the stairwell!"

He poked his head back out the door. Mucker had a metal prong between his teeth and was making rapid circles with a chicken bone in his right hand and an unlit candle in his left.

"All I'm saying," came a second voice from the stairwell, "is that I'm glad we got assigned watch duty instead of wolf duty. Did you see Griffin's arm?"

"Fair enough," agreed the first. Their voices were getting clearer as they neared.

"Psst," Spike hissed.

Sweat dripped from Mucker's brow as he worked. His eyes darted from the stairwell behind him to the task at hand. "Almost there," he rasped—although the sound he actually made with his teeth clenched around a tool was more like *Uhgust ehr*.

Spike pulled his head back inside the storeroom. "Only a couple of them," he whispered to Drusilla. "Shouldn't be too much trouble."

"Scores," Drusilla whispered back.

"Mm? No, it sounds like only two. They don't seem to know we're here yet, so if we keep quiet, we'll have the jump on them."

"Miss Edith says there are scores of them."

Spike eyed the doll warily. "Miss Edith's eyes are painted on. I'm pretty sure it's just two."

A sudden movement at the door caught their attention. Mucker hustled into the room, stuffing his tool roll back inside his coat. He slid the door closed but for the slimmest crack, and then pressed his back to the wall and a finger to his lips.

Spike nodded. There were only a couple of guards against the three of them—and they had the element of surprise. This would be quick work. Could be fun, even.

Out of the corner of his eye, a sparkle of light caught his attention. The reliquary was still sitting there, its box glistening invitingly. Spike swallowed.

Things were about to start happening very quickly, and when things happened quickly, plans had a tendency to change at a moment's notice. Maybe they would spring Ears from his cell, precisely as they had planned—but maybe they would have to leg it without him. Come what may, there was no chance Spike was going to let that sodding pinkie get left behind in the excitement. He had promised. He tiptoed across the room to nab it before the melee broke out.

What are you doing? Mucker mouthed furiously.

Spike ignored him. He reached across the table.

Outside the door, the voices grew even louder. "I knew a lizard demon who lost her arm once." The guards had reached the final landing. The sound of their footsteps neared the door. "I mean, she grew a new one, of course, but it was never the same. She was always sort of lopsided after that."

Spike's fingers closed on the ornate reliquary, and—in the pregnant silence of the treasure room—the hiss of burning flesh was audible.

It took everything Spike had not to yelp in pain. Silver. *Church* silver. Spike cursed himself silently and pulled back his hand. His elbow thudded against a fancy plinth as he withdrew, and—with horror, he saw the heavy bronze bell topple over.

The world around him slowed as Spike reached to catch it, but he was not fast enough. The rim of the bell struck the floor with . . .

Absolute silence.

Spike froze.

The thick bell bounced off the floor hard enough to chip the marble—but it did so with all the resonance of a feather striking linen. Spike blinked at the artifact as it rolled to a noiseless stop by his foot. He patted his own ears. Had he gone deaf? All sound had died away. He strained to hear the footsteps of the approaching guards, but only resounding silence filled the chamber. Abruptly, the door swung open, and Spike found himself still standing in the middle of the room, face-to-face with a chaos demon.

CHAPTER TWENTY-ONE

The chaos demon froze mid-step, eyes wide. His bulky frame blocked most of the doorway into the treasure room, but Spike could see the hem of a gray dress behind him. Just two guards. The vampires could handle two demon guards easily. Granted, the chaos demon gawking down at him was more of an opponent and a half. The brute was at least seven feet tall, even before taking into account his slimy antlers, which dripped soundlessly onto the lapels of his suit.

He and Spike stared at each other for several seconds. And then the demon's brain apparently caught up with his eyes, and he opened his mouth to bellow . . . except not a whisper escaped his lips. The pure, eerie silence continued, unbroken. What the sodding hell was going on?

Did you do this? Spike mouthed at the chaos demon.

The demon put a hand to his own throat, confused, and shook his head.

Beyond him, Spike could see the etchings covering the nearest cell door had gone dark. Ah. Ears was free and clearly putting his auditory manipulation to use. Excellent. So Mucker had finished the job before cowering around the corner, then. Maybe the bastard was good for something after all.

The chaos demon, having gotten over his initial startlement, scowled and charged, ducking his head to fit his dripping antlers through the door. Spike rolled out of his way easily, scooping up the heavy bell by its handle as he did. By the time the demon had straightened and spun to face him, Spike was already mid-swing.

The thick bronze bell connected with the demon's temple with enough force to send both of them reeling. The bell vibrated mutely in Spike's hand for several seconds as the demon crashed into the nearest table, sending glistening coins and gems scattering across the floor. He pushed himself back up, but the table gave way beneath his weight, and at once, a bevy of priceless rarities cascaded onto the brute, all with surreal noiselessness. As antique vases and wooden chests bounced off the demon's antlers, the memory of tinkling harpsichord music began to play in the back of Spike's mind.

Spike had always appreciated a good slapstick routine. A handful of years ago, Angelus had treated the fanged four to a moving-picture show in Paris—a comedy about two melodramatic actors fighting over a swooning leading lady. The whole thing had culminated in a vaudevillian fight, complete with custard pies and bursting flour sacks, all accompanied by an upbeat ditty. Everyone in the theater had enjoyed a good laugh, Drusilla had held his hand, the audience had died screaming, and the harpsichord player had tasted faintly of rum. Simpler times. Spike smiled at the memory as the chaos demon floundered in front of him.

A flash of movement brought him back to the present, and

Spike spun around in time to see the second guard charge into the room. Plum-colored leathery wings tucked themselves tight against her sides as she dove forward. Mucker, the cowardly tit, pressed himself tighter against the wall, and the demon shot straight past him.

Drusilla, on the other hand, met the hellion in the air.

One arm still clutching Ed's vessel, Drusilla drove her free fist into the jaw of the succubus. Vampire and demon spiraled hard into a wall like two blackbirds colliding soundlessly mid-flight. The demon whipped her wine-dark tail at Drusilla, but the vampire skipped over it like she was jumping rope in a schoolyard. The succubus kicked, but Drusilla was a blur. She pirouetted out of the way, returning the attack with a knee to the demon's ribs and a backhand to her face. The demon tottered on her feet, recoiling from the assault.

Drusilla's cheeks dimpled as her wide smile revealed a savage set of fangs. If Spike had still had a heartbeat, it almost certainly would have skipped at the sight. He could watch Drusilla fight all night.

Unfortunately, with his attention on the skirmish in front of him, he was *not* watching the chaos demon behind him, who was finally pulling himself out of the mess and rising to his feet. A tingle up Spike's spine made him turn his head—but just a second too late. The wind rushed out of him as the demon's punch drove hard into his gut. Clumsily, Spike swung the bell again, but this time, the brute caught him by the wrist. Spike felt his momentum betray him as the demon yanked his arm to one side, throwing Spike off his feet. He skidded on a pile of loose coins and landed roughly on his stomach, the cold marble slapping him across the face. He shook his head and blinked.

Directly in front of him was the remains of a shattered glass box with ornate silver metalwork along its sides. Within it was the notable absence of a shriveled pinkie finger. Spike scrambled to his knees and glanced around frantically. The pinkie. It had to be here somewhere!

A shadow fell over him, and he looked up to see a set of glistening antlers coming at him at great speed.

Those who have not had occasion to encounter a chaos demon in person may not be aware that the viscous slime secreted from their horns is sticky and syrupy, and smells faintly like toasted coconut. For a brief period in the 1890s, a chaos demon by the name of Nicophet even marketed his own antler slime as Naughty Nick's Hair Treatment, finding some success in the North American market. The slime's mild intoxicating quality, however, proved to induce unexpected side effects when massaged directly into the scalp over prolonged periods of time. As a result, after their slow decline into madness, the product's most loyal customer base stopped purchasing enough tins to keep the business afloat. Clinical insanity aside, the treatment had been otherwise regarded as a thoroughly pleasant experience.

Spike might not have been ideally positioned to appreciate the warm, tropical undertones of the antler slime as the two of them thundered out the storeroom door and back onto the landing. The mucus squished under Spike's grip as he twisted, trying to get control of himself before the demon's blind, head-down charge drove them both straight into a wall. He could still feel the weight of the bell in one hand, but he couldn't contort himself into a position to swing it effectively. Out of the corner of one eye, he saw the pale purple figure of Ermack dive out of the way, and then, suddenly, the chaos demon planted his feet and lurched to a stop. Spike clutched fruitlessly at the gooey prongs with his free hand as he felt himself go airborne. He landed hard on one knee and rolled until his back hit a wall. The bell bounced out of his grip and spun to a stop in the corner.

Spike's back ached. Stiffly, he pushed himself up to sitting. He had landed in a small square room about seven feet wide with a low ceiling and brick walls—Ermack's empty cell. His ears were ringing. Wait. Scratch that. It was the bell that was reverberating, its toll slowly fading away. Spike could hear again. Gradually, sound was creeping back to his ears—and with it a clomping of heavy footsteps. He looked up at the cell door as the chaos demon leaned down, cracking his neck and flexing his muscles.

"Didn't anybody ever tell you?" the demon said, a sneer playing across his lips. "You mess with Azerom, you get the horns!"

"Really?" Spike raised an eyebrow. "That's what you're going with?"

Azerom hesitated. "Oh. I—I didn't actually know the sound was back on." He cleared his throat. "I had a better one earlier about you being in a *sticky* situation, but I don't think anybody heard it."

"I'm sure we all missed out," said Spike.

Without warning, the demon's eyes suddenly went round and he flew forward, antlers clacking off the doorframe as he pitched wildly into the cell. Spike rolled out of the way moments before Azerom's forehead hit the bricks with a dull crunch. When Spike looked up, Drusilla was standing on the demon's back, a splash of dark burgundy blood on her cheek and a baby doll still cradled under one arm.

"Hello, my love," she crooned. "Hope you don't mind me cutting in. I broke mine."

"Always happy to share." Spike gave Azerom's head a nudge with his toe. The demon let out a raspy moan but did not get up. "I think you broke this one, too."

"I got excited." Drusilla smiled in that special way that would've made Spike's knees go weak if they weren't already bruised to bits. "What's that?" she said, putting her ear close to the doll again. "What—him? The one with all the slime? Miss Edith, you are naughty."

Spike pushed himself up to his feet. "Ironically, I think we have the Dread Lord of London Town to thank for how easily our sticky friend here went down. Ordinary bricks would've cracked to dust under a good, hard demon skull like his, so I expect that's part of the special reinforcements Gunnar paid for."

Mucker's nervous face appeared in the doorway, peeking in cautiously.

"We're fine," Spike said. "In fact, I'm starting to believe we might actually pull this off. I'm not entirely used to things going according to plan."

"About that . . ." said Mucker. And then the cell door slammed shut.

CHAPTER TWENTY-TWO

Through the window of the cramped cell, Spike could see Mucker's face lit from below as the inscriptions on the metal began to glow again. He raced to the door and slammed against it, but he might as well have been trying to budge a mountain. He and Drusilla were sealed up tight in a magical prison with bonds too strong for even a full-grown mountain troll to bust through. Glaring daggers at the grubby vampire, Spike pounded on the window with a fist. "What the hell are you playing at?" he yelled. "The plan was *working*, you gormless nit. You're cocking up a nearly finished job!"

"Oh, the plan is still working." Mucker tapped on the glass with a dirty fingernail. "Just not *your* plan."

Beside him, a very confused Ears looked from Spike's scowling face to Mucker and back again. "Are they—*not* on our side?"

"They had their role to play," Mucker informed him. "And they played it. This was always the endgame. Sometimes to get the checkmate you've got to sacrifice a knight or two."

"You absolute knuckle," Spike hissed. "You couldn't win a game of chess against a goldfish. Or haven't you noticed—you still need this particular pair of knights to get you pathetic pawns out of here."

"What we needed," corrected Mucker, "were a couple of patsies. You're doing great, by the way. Keep it up. I especially liked the part where you basically locked yourselves up for me, really considerate of you."

Spike shot him a glare that could have welded steel. "Who's *we*?" he demanded.

Mucker looked confused.

"You just said *we*, so you didn't come up with this big-boy villain move by yourself. Was it Hammond's idea? Was this the plan all along? You and I both know you haven't got the fangs to take a bite this big on your own."

"You act like you're so much better than me," Mucker spat.

"It's only acting if it's not true," said Spike.

"Oh yeah? Is that why you're in a box and I'm out here? *Mm?* I won. You lost."

Spike glared daggers at the grubby vampire. Mucker tipped his derby in mock civility at the cell window.

"Not to sound ungrateful," Ermack cut in, "but I can definitely hear feet starting to climb the stairs. A lot of them. Too many of them. I appreciate you coming back for me, but how exactly are we planning to get out of this tower?"

Spike crossed his arms and raised his eyebrows. "Well?" he said. "Answer the bloke. How are you, a weaseling little plonker, gonna get the two of you out of this house *without* our help?"

"Through the front door," said Mucker, not the least bit fussed. "At our leisure, thank you very much. Game's already over. I won."

He leaned against the banister to wait, calmly picking at his fingernails. He glanced at Ermack, who was beginning to pace anxiously. "Don't you worry your pretty periwinkle head. Everything is under control. Trust me."

"You mean like *we* trusted him?" Spike said to Ermack through the glass. "Look how well that turned out."

Ermack looked far from confident, but he stood behind Mucker as the sound of feet marching up the stairs grew louder and louder. There had to be dozens of demons this time. Maybe more.

Spike ground his teeth. This was bad. He looked back at Drusilla, who seemed blissfully unfazed by their hopeless predicament. With one toe, she was gently tracing the edges of the dark flagstones that formed the floor of the cell.

It wasn't fair. For once, Spike had made a plan. He had been patient. He had done everything right. And yet, as always, here they were with nothing to show for it in the end—and he was stuck trying to sort out how to make that *nothing* somehow work. He clenched his jaw and turned back to the window.

"Mucker. You don't want to do this," he growled.

"What do I not want to do? Hand you over to an army of demons who will gladly make garlands out of your guts?" Mucker answered. "No, actually, you would be surprised how much I really do want to do that."

The demons stomped up onto the landing two at a time, horns, scales, thorns, and tails filling what little space there was between Mucker and the top of the stairs in mere moments. Near the front were the pair who had fallen for the haunted-doll trick, black-eyed Sisseroth and his spiny-faced partner. Plenty more of them awaited farther down. Twenty altogether? Thirty? It was impossible to see from Spike's cell window.

"Took you long enough," Mucker mumbled as they filed in and shuffled to a stop.

Sisseroth stepped to the head of the group, tinted glasses still covering his eyes. He had not yet replaced his ruined necktie, and his complexion looked even more ashen than usual. "He's in there?" he hissed.

"And his gonzo girl, too," Mucker confirmed. "Two-for-one special."

Sisseroth edged forward until he met Spike's gaze through the glass, and then his face cracked into a spiteful smile. "I wasn't sure you were stupid enough to actually try it, blood rat." He stepped closer to the cell. "I'm glad you were, though. I'm looking forward to making sure you regret it."

Spike rolled his eyes. "You're just grumpy because I tied you to that guy with a face like a durian."

"Hey," said Durian Face from the front of the horde.

"I've always thought of him more as a pineapple," Sisseroth mused. "But either way, that definitely didn't win you any points."

"Um. My name is Travis," said Durian Face. "I'm a Brachen demon."

"Shut up, Travis," growled a rumbling voice behind him. The throng parted, and Gunnar himself stalked forward. The big red gorilla of a demon eyed Mucker, who did not straighten up per se but did shift to a slightly more attentive slouch. "About time you earned your paycheck," Gunnar grunted.

"With interest," Mucker answered with all the charm of a secondhand carriage salesman. "Didn't I tell you I could help you trade in this lavender lesser for a bigger catch? I present to you the slayer killer himself, plus one sadistic seer with a few screws loose. There's not a nastier pair of vampires in all Europe."

"You're gonna make me blush," Spike said through the glass.

Mucker ignored him. "They're all yours, Gunnar. Packed up neat and tidy in one of your own cells. I didn't get the Kakophonos dampener back in place, but you don't need that anymore anyway, and the standard binding will more than hold a pair of vampires, even a pair like them. Did everything but pin the ribbon on top of the present. You're welcome. Oh—you might want to drag that fellow with the antlers out of there, if you get the chance."

Gunnar leaned in close to get a look at Spike and Drusilla. "I did warn you." He tutted. "I mean, I was hoping you'd try something anyway, but I did warn you. Nice of you to bring the missus along this time." He cocked his head to one side. "What's she doing?"

Spike looked over his shoulder. Drusilla appeared blissfully unaware of the developments taking place outside the cell and was playfully balancing on one foot at a time, moving from stone to stone like she was in the middle of a game of hopscotch.

"She's . . . quirky," Spike said. "It's charming."

"Know what's not so charming? Half a dozen busted-up guards, a broken window downstairs, plus a pile of demolished antiquities in my treasure room." Gunnar shook his head. "You know I don't like it when people touch my things, Spike."

"You should really talk to your meddling minions about that," said Spike. "We were actually being uncharacteristically delicate until they blundered in. In fact, there's no telling what sort of damage they might have caused if we hadn't been here to stop them. Consider it a service rendered. We'll bill you later."

Gunnar clicked his tongue. "You disappointed me, slayer killer."

"Disappointing people is one of the many things I'm good at," Spike replied. "Right after being rakishly good-looking and just before balancing a cocktail glass on one finger."

"I offered you a chance to put your talents to good use," Gunnar continued, "and you decided to steal from me."

"Oh, come off it." Spike rolled his eyes. "You know you had it coming."

"Who—me?" Gunnar looked shocked. "I'm not the one who busted into this house and broke all those beautiful things. I was having a perfectly peaceful night. I took a walk. Organized the torture hooks in the dungeon. Did some stretches. I even treated myself to two lumps in my cuppa earlier."

"Lumps of what?"

"Liver, I think. Maybe kidney. Cook whipped it up. It was a real nice touch."

"Well, I'd love to let you get back to all that, so if you don't mind popping these old arcane charms, we'll be out from under your cloven feet in two shakes of a sacrificial lamb's tail."

Gunnar laughed and turned his back on the window.

"Don't look at me," Mucker said. "I just delivered the chatty sod. What you do with him is up to you."

"Okay, half-breed," said Gunnar, "where were we?"

Drusilla sniffed the air and skipped across the cell until she was next to Spike. She slid her arm under his and leaned her chin on his shoulder. "Ooh," she said. "I think it's about to happen."

"What's about to happen?" said Spike, but the whole of Drusilla's attention was now on the narrow window.

"Been a pleasure," the treacherous Mucker was saying. "But I'm gonna get back to my *other* employer now. Only thing I like more than gettin' paid is gettin' paid *twice*. And I do believe my cut for bringing home Hammond's little purple pal here just went up." He shot Spike and Drusilla a self-satisfied smile. "Ta."

Gunnar slapped a hand on Ermack's shoulder as the trembling

Kakophonos demon attempted to follow Mucker. Ermack looked like he might crumple under the weight.

"Not so fast," said Gunnar.

Mucker hesitated. "Funny joke," he said, giving a half-hearted laugh. Gunnar wasn't smiling. Mucker swallowed. "We had a deal."

"We *did*," said Gunnar, nodding thoughtfully. "But the trouble is, I find myself in possession of *three* rather powerful trophies right now, and you're attempting to leave me with only *two* of them. Can't have that. It's about principles, see? I've got this policy—it's real simple: If something belongs to me, I don't let it go."

"But we had a contract," Mucker said. "You're a demon. There's rules. You can't just break a contract."

"Right you are, my greasy friend. But while you most certainly do have a contract with *me*"—Gunnar nodded toward the army of demons behind him—"I don't believe you have any such deal with *them*. And I have a feeling they might not take kindly to a lowly gutter vamp forcing their venerable Dread Lord of London Town to give up a hard-earned trophy if they can do anything about it. Isn't that right?"

There were wicked chuckles and grunts of agreement from the crowd. "*I* would certainly be forced to object," Sisseroth hissed behind Mucker's ear. "Firmly."

The last remnants of Mucker's smug smile completely fell away. He swallowed hard, the weight of his precarious position finally settling over him like a soggy blanket. "Fair enough." He managed a nervous chuckle. "I know when I'm snookered. You win. Keep him. I'll go." He tried to back away, but the only exits were a four-story drop or a wall of demons.

Ermack was visibly shaking under Gunnar's grip.

"And leave red in my ledger?" said Gunnar with mock dismay. "If I let you walk out of here empty-handed, I would owe you. Me, a respectable demon, owing you, a filthy vampire. Can you imagine? You're right—we had a deal. As I recall, our contract is binding until satisfied . . . or until death." The corners of his mouth pricked up. "Can't run a top-notch criminal syndicate if I go around owing debts to every dirty rat running free in my city, now can I?"

"So, what are you gonna do?" Mucker croaked. "Make a trophy out of me, too? Stick me in one of your cells?" His eyes flicked to the narrow window through which Spike and Drusilla were still viewing the scene. A funny expression crossed Mucker's face as he locked eyes with Drusilla. She squeezed Spike's arm like a kid watching a magic trick.

"Nope," grunted Gunnar. "That's for *worthy* adversaries." And with no further warning, a metallic blade, something between a longsword and a javelin, erupted from Gunnar's wrist. His muscles flexed and the blade carved a clean arc through the air, vanishing back into his arm as quickly as it had sprouted. The entire motion had taken less than a second. For a demon built like a bull, Gunnar moved with lighting speed.

For several moments, Mucker just stared numbly ahead, his wide eyes still locked on Drusilla's. And then his head tipped back, and his body tipped forward. The head drifted apart into a trail of ashy dust until there was nothing left but the tattered derby fluttering down the long drop toward the bottom of the stairs. The corpse hit the ground with a less graceful *whump*, disintegrating at once into a filthy cloud that spilled across the stairwell.

Several demons near the front began to cough.

"Ugh, he got everywhere," said Gunnar. "I'm going to be cleaning vampire dust off these stairs for ages. Could somebody go grab a broom? Travis? Thanks." He turned back to Ermack. Ermack paled. "Don't worry, pipsqueak," Gunnar said. "I haven't forgotten about you."

CHAPTER TWENTY-THREE

Gunnar looked as if he could have ground the pale purple Ermack under his heel. The Kakophonos demon swallowed nervously as his captor squared up in front of him.

"I could have sworn I told you to stay put," Gunnar said, rubbing his chin. "Of course, it's possible you didn't hear me. I do seem to recall there was a lot of *noise*. Maybe you need to hear it again." He let the wicked metallic blade slide very slowly from his wrist again. Spike had next to no experience with Hastam demons, but he could tell even through the thick glass that the demonic weapon held a razor-sharp edge. Gunnar let the blade caress the front of Ermack's tunic. "I'll have to say it more . . . *slowly* this time," Gunnar purred.

Spike felt a tug on his arm.

"You're in the wrong spot, my sweet," said Drusilla. "Can't dance over the corpses if you don't learn the steps."

"We're locked in a box, Dru," said Spike. "Not much room for dancing."

"Not yet," said Drusilla. "Soon. Stand right . . . here. No, wait. Here."

Spike sighed, but he allowed Drusilla to navigate him a few feet closer to the wall. His foot nudged the bronze bell, and it tinkled against the bricks, the noise echoing softly in the tiny chamber.

"Remember," Drusilla said, brushing Spike's cheek with one hand, "the four of cups. You've got to lean into it."

"*Lean into*— What is that supposed to mean?"

Outside the cell, Gunnar was still talking. "Well?" he demanded. "Anything to say for yourself?"

"J-just one thing," Ermack stammered.

Drusilla spun away from Spike like a ballet dancer, pirouetting until both of her feet stopped on a wide stone slab near the back of the cell. She closed her eyes and rocked up and down on the balls of her feet, like a gymnast getting ready to perform her routine.

"The bell," Ermack said evenly.

"What?" Gunnar grunted.

"The bell," Ermack repeated, more loudly. "Use the bell!"

"Have you gone nutty already? I haven't even started the torture yet. What bell are you on about?" Gunnar shook his head, but then his gaze turned toward the pile of artifacts in the next room. In another moment, he whipped around to face the cell. His eyes went wide.

Spike finally caught on. He scooped up the Jericho Doorbell and raised it over his head. Ermack closed his eyes, his brow knitting in concentration. Drusilla put her fingers in her ears.

Spike rang the bell.

There are noises so loud that they hop the tracks of hearing and blunder their way onto the rails of the other senses—noises so loud they seem blinding—noises so loud they feel almost tangible.

The concussive gong that resonated just above Spike's head was loud enough to physically slap him off his feet and leave a foul taste in his mouth.

He threw his hands over his ears as he hit the ground, and a moment later, the bell struck the floor beside him with a second deafening ring, and then a third and fourth as it bounced to a stop. Spike could hear nothing but the bell. He was swimming in a terrible ocean of sound, and every new peal was like another merciless wave crashing over his head. Barely able to think, he squeezed his eyes shut. His whole body was shaking so hard he could scarcely keep his hands clapped over his tortured ears. Slowly, the sound began fading—well, not fading so much as transforming from a measurable volume into a numb pain that lived within his skull. With tremendous force of will, he opened his eyes.

The charmed, immovable bricks . . . had shifted. It looked as if someone had blown up a giant invisible balloon right in the center of the room and pressed each wall ever so slightly outward. The force had not been enough to actually blast down any of the walls, sadly—that would have been asking too much of his luck. The shaking, wobbly sensation still running through him, Spike realized, was not his body, but the tower itself. The floor was shuddering as the whole place rumbled with aftershocks of the sonic blast.

Drusilla, her expression pinched and her fingers still in her ears, kicked the chaos demon Azerom over so that his body flopped onto the bell, and finally the sound abated. Spike lowered his hands gingerly from the sides of his head. The only ringing was now in his eardrums.

From beyond the door came the sound of a deep voice yelling furiously, followed by a crash and then more shouting. Everything sounded muffled, as if Spike had his head underwater and was listening to people holler into pillows high above him. Dizzily, he pushed himself up to his feet.

The scene through the narrow window of the cell was absolute chaos. He could see starlight twinkling through a gaping hole on the far side of the tower, and there were streams of dust and debris trickling from above. A chunk of masonry the size of a wine barrel smashed down from the ceiling, taking out a stretch of the banister beside Ermack. The horde of demons were attempting to scatter. The general consensus appeared to be *go down, get out*, but the larger demons on the highest landing were trying to make their exit over the bodies of the smaller demons below them, leading to a roiling pile of horns and claws, kicking and fighting as they tumbled down the rapidly collapsing steps. A few winged demons had taken flight and made it through the widening hole in the wall, but as Spike watched, a succubus making the attempt caught a falling rafter to the wing and spun out, careening down the stairwell instead of into the open air.

The ashen-faced Sisseroth had braced himself in the doorway to the treasure room to ride out the tremors, but—with a crackling that sounded as if it were echoing up to Spike from the bottom of a deep well—the ceiling split open and the stonework around Sisseroth fell to pieces. The sneering gargoyle above him dropped straight down, and with a dull crunch, the place on the demon's shoulders where his head should have been was suddenly replaced by a heavy stone animal covered in something dark and sticky. His body swayed for a moment and then collapsed to the ground.

Any decent human being with a scrap of empathy would have been traumatized by the sight. Spike stifled a giggle.

Gunnar, his face an even brighter shade of red than usual, shot a murderous glare through the cell window before vaulting over what was left of Sisseroth and into the storeroom. The whole floor tilted suddenly, and Spike felt himself go weightless for a moment as the floor dropped away beneath him—and then, just as quickly, his feet slammed back down again. The scene beyond the window was suddenly spinning. The stronghold was collapsing.

Even as the tower fell apart around it, the enchantment on the cell was straining to remain intact. Dark stones were clinging to one another by virtue of magic alone as the cell pitched and shuddered, but with every lurching shift, the masonry fell apart a little more. Spike briefly had time to consider that the occult charm designed to entrap them might actually be the one thing keeping them safe as the rest of the building crumbled right on top of the retreating demon horde.

The ground fell away again, and this time Spike bounced from the floor to the ceiling. They tilted, and after a jarring ride, he found himself lying with his back against what had been a wall only moments before. A stone from the opposite side of the cell finally lost its magical grip and came loose, smashing a path straight through the brickwork half a foot to the right of Spike's head. Moments later, another one cannonballed across the cell and shattered through the bricks an inch to his left. Spike swallowed. Had he moved a matter of inches in either direction, his head would have been a match to Sisseroth's.

Across from him, Drusilla ducked her chin to her chest calmly a fraction of a second before a timber came crashing through the wall above her like a battering ram. She caught Spike's eye and shot him a wink. The two of them were being rattled like ice cubes in a cocktail shaker, and yet they were miraculously missing the worst of the damage.

No, Spike realized. Not miraculously. *This* was why Drusilla had insisted he stand just so. Her precognitive positioning had saved him from having his skull caved in. Maybe, against all odds, they would get out of this unharmed. The cell lurched again, and a handful of debris pelted Spike's face. He raised an arm to block the onslaught, and almost at once, his shoulder slammed into something solid, sending him ricocheting between slabs of stone that seemed to be emerging from nowhere. So much for unharmed.

Spike blinked dust out of his eyes. The four walls of the cell were in shambles now, the crumbling power of the enchantment doing its damnedest to keep the few remaining sections from completely giving up on one another, but every side was riddled with missing and broken bricks. The ceiling had been torn away completely. The face of a very uncomfortable-looking Fyarl demon smashed against the window of the cell door and left a smeary streak as it was scraped away. A battered chest bounced through the open ceiling and shattered near Spike's foot. Out tumbled several shiny necklaces, goblets, and coins. Spike shook his head and tried to find his balance.

And then, once more, they were weightless.

Spike felt his stomach rise to his chest. In the air in front of him, a handful of coins and four glittering goblets spun slowly upward. Spike blinked. Four cups. What was he supposed to do with four cups?

At the last second before they came dashing back down to the ground, Spike leaned in.

The world went black.

In the indistinguishable roar of sounds, he felt a sharp pain rip across his whole left side, felt his body slam to a stop, and felt the crush of stone and wood pressing down on him from above.

And then . . .

. . . at last . . .

. . . everything was still.

Spike's ears were still ringing and his eyes stung. A suffocating cloud of masonry dust hung over everything. He coughed. If breathing had been an absolute necessity and not simply a fond habit, Spike might have been in real trouble. He tried to sit up, and his rib cage exploded with pain. Blindly, he reached a hand up to his chest.

A shard of wood as thick as his forearm—likely splintered off of some joist or ruptured rafter—had pierced clean through his back and out of his rib cage. He'd been staked! After everything else he had been through, the sodding tower had staked him! It had nearly done the job, too—missed his heart by a finger's width. If he hadn't been leaning into those bloody cups when it happened, the cloud of dust hanging in the air right now would be *him*.

Spike reached up and felt smooth, cold metal above him. With an agonizing shove, he moved aside the remains of the door. Its etchings had, at last, gone completely dark. Rocks and debris settled around him as the door clunked aside. In the space he had made, he carefully slid himself off the jagged stake with a faint squelching sound. Clumsily, he felt above him again. He pushed, shifting the detritus piece by piece as he made his way up. A few bricks and a large section of tiled roof later, Spike felt the rush of fresh air above him. Painfully, he pulled himself to his feet, shaking dust and pebbles out of his hair as he looked out over the remains of Gunnar's mansion on Wych Street.

The buildings to either side of the mansion were still standing, but they looked as if they had survived a bomb blast. They had missing shingles and broken windows, and a long section of trim was dangling from the nearest roof like a pendulum. Lights were flickering on in a few neighboring windows already.

A short ways away, a pile of bricks clattered as it shifted, and a greenish hand emerged. Spike watched as it clawed its way upward, dragging a red-haired troll up into the moonlight. The brute shook himself off and did not spare so much as a glance backward before bounding off into the night. Out of the corner of his eye, Spike thought he might have seen a creature like a fiery chimpanzee scaling the drainpipe of a neighboring building before disappearing onto the rooftops. So at least a few of the other captives had been freed by the demolition, too. He hadn't intended to turn the mission into a wholesale jailbreak, but he had certainly broken the jail.

Footsteps clicked against the rubble behind him, and Spike turned to spot Drusilla. She appeared completely unscathed, save for a fine coating of plaster dust that clung to her hair and her elegant dress. Unbelievably, she was even still holding the ridiculous baby doll.

"Spike!" She threw herself into his arms, and Spike grunted as the hole in his rib cage blossomed in pain. She pulled back, concern playing across her eyes. "Are you all right, my pet?"

"Only a punctured lung," he wheezed. "I'll be right as rot in no time."

Drusilla wrapped an arm around his neck and smiled contentedly. Spike leaned into her. "You were right," she whispered.

"I was?" he managed. "About what?"

"We're not the tower." She giggled. "We're the flames."

CHAPTER TWENTY-FOUR

Eddies of dust swirled over the mound that had once been Gunnar's terrible tower. Spike's ears were ringing, but somewhere within the whine, he caught a scratching, clawing sound. By the time he pinpointed its source, the surface of the heap churned, and a figure erupted from a mess of plaster and splintered wood.

Spike tensed, sending a pulse of sharp pain bouncing from his chest to his extremities. The figure was facing away from them, but Spike could plainly see it wasn't Gunnar. The creature was ghostly white, wearing tattered dark robes. Not one of his goons, then, either. Spike relaxed, sending another shock of pain rattling around his body.

"Ahh!" The pallid man reached out his palms as if caressing the cool air. "I am liberated at long last from my wretched prison—once more free to stalk the accursed night!" He turned his milky-white bald head to the star-strewn heavens. Even before the figure had noticed them, Spike caught the scent of rotten cabbage in the air.

Spike's eyebrows rose. "Count Orlok?"

Orlok spun, fixing his sunken eyes on Spike and Drusilla. "You!" The missing member of the London Vampires' Guild pointed his finger—like a gnarled white root—toward them. "I know you, young ones."

"Well, yeah," said Spike. "We've met."

"I think I borrowed your butler to write my name in the book," said Drusilla.

"Ah yes, but of course. I see you plainly now. You are the nefarious brood of my most delectable lady, Darla." His eyes brightened hopefully as he glanced around.

"She's my grandmother," said Drusilla.

"She's not here," said Spike. "Sorry, mate. I'll tell her you said hello."

Orlok looked only mildly disappointed. "You two fiends of darkness have done this thing on your own?" He gestured at the ruination surrounding them.

"Erm. Yep." Spike looked at Dru. "I guess so. More or less. There was a demon involved who wasn't entirely useless."

"You have risked much to free me, I am sure." Orlok nodded contemplatively. "The unholy service you have rendered this night will long be remembered." And then he whipped his tattered robes around and, with a whoosh, vanished into black smoke. The dust whirled and spun as it followed his passing, and soon all that remained of Count Orlok atop the ruins was a lingering cabbage scent.

"Did you know he was locked up in the tower?" asked Drusilla.

"Nope," said Spike. "Why is it only the really obnoxious vampires get the extra-special powers? I could have a lot of fun with turning into smoke or becoming a bat or something."

The two of them began to pick their way across the wreckage when a deep voice cut through the fog and dust. "Funny. I do not remember the plan involving leveling a bloody building." Spike squinted into the haze until he could make out Hammond stepping over rubble as he cut a path across Wych Street. Rieka skipped past him, making her way up the mountain of debris.

"Sure it was," Spike managed hoarsely. His voice sounded odd in his own head. Even with vampiric accelerated healing, his eardrums were still recovering from all the excitement. "Remember the bit at the end of the plan where we said if things went fangs-up, we would have to improvise? Well. Ta-da."

"This was Ermack's doing," said Rieka, "wasn't it?"

"Well, yeah, mostly," Spike admitted. "But I helped."

Rieka sniffed the air and then immediately sneezed from a cloud of plaster dust. "Where is he?" she managed.

Spike gestured broadly at the rubble. "Down?" he suggested.

"Bloody demons." Hammond shook his head. "When they go all out, they don't muck about, do they?"

"Your mate Mucker didn't leave us with a lot of options," Spike said.

"I heard," Hammond groaned. "Ed told us what happened— that treacherous little cockroach."

"And what did Ed tell you, exactly?" said Spike.

"That he double-crossed ya. Ruined the plan."

"You sure that wasn't the plan all along?" Spike said. His eyelids narrowed. "Got to give the greasy git some credit. Trading me and Dru to get your werewolf's boysenberry boyfriend back wasn't a bad idea, really. Could have done the trick. Almost beyond Mucker to have come up with it on his own."

Hammond waved the accusation away. "You know I don't work like that," he said. "Who helped smuggle you and Angelus out the back door of that coven back in eighty-two? Coulda got myself a pretty penny for each of your heads if I had turned you over the minute you was out. But I didn't, did I? No. Because we vampires got to stick together."

"Somebody should've told Mucker that," Spike grumbled.

"*She's* not a vampire," said Drusilla, her eyes on Rieka, who had begun pawing through the debris, her nose still twitching.

"No," Spike agreed. "She's not."

Rieka seemed to feel Spike's gaze on the back of her head. She straightened and turned, fixing Spike with a long stare. "Really? I went along with your idiot plan. I let them think I intended to betray you, I acted all surprised when Hammond offered me instead, and then I took on half a dozen demons single-handedly while you parasites were playing hide-and-seek—once again carrying this entire team on my shoulders—and now you're seriously going to give *me* the stink eye?"

"He said *we*." Spike squared his shoulders at the werewolf.

"What?"

"Mucker. He said *we* needed patsies. Not *I*." Spike watched her expression carefully. "He was working with someone else to sell us out. Be honest, of the crew, *you're* the only one who literally has two faces. *You're* the only one with no clan loyalty to anyone else in the group—other than whatever it is between you and Ears."

Rieka raised an eyebrow. "Let's get one thing absolutely clear, bloodsucker. I *would* happily trade you for Ermack. I would do it right now. Hell, if you're insisting on honesty, I would probably trade you for a plate of fish and chips, if they did the chips just a little crunchy, the way I like them. But rest assured, the day I decide to screw you, you'll know without a doubt who's turning the screws."

"No flirting," said Drusilla. "Unless I'm invited."

Spike eyed Rieka for a beat but then nodded, mollified for the time being.

"If you're all done leveling accusations," Hammond said, "I'd say it's well past time we clear out." He peered up and down the street. More lights had flicked on in the neighboring buildings, and faces were peering out of windows to try to see what was going on. Bells were clanging several blocks away.

"Not without Ermack," said Rieka.

Hammond sighed. "Two minutes," he conceded. He turned back to Spike and Drusilla. "You two go reunite Ed with her vessel. Then I think it's best you make like a Thesulac demon."

Drusilla's face brightened with interest. "You mean whisper terrible secrets to our victims until they go mad?"

"I mean *vanish*," clarified Hammond. "Make like a Thesulac and *vanish*. You should get out of here."

Drusilla looked mildly disappointed, but she nodded. "I suppose that does make more sense in this situation," she said.

Before they could part ways, a sound caught Rieka's ear and her head shot up. Following a muffled voice beneath the wreckage, she began pitching bricks aside. Spike peered over her shoulder to watch. The voice grew louder and louder as she worked. Finally, muscles straining, she heaved a wide slab of broken granite over her head, revealing a face below.

"Hooray!" Cricklewood breathed. The demon doorman had a gash across his forehead and a bloody lip. "I'm saved!"

"Ugh." Rieka rolled her eyes and dropped the slab back where she had found it. "Where *is* he?"

"I'm sure he's under here somewhere," Spike said. "Dropping a house on a demon never tends to stop them for long. Hammond's right. We need to get out of this place fast. I'd rather not *exit pursued by a barreling horde of demons*, if I can avoid it. I have it on good authority that the self-styled Dread Lord of London Town doesn't like it when people mess with his things."

"And you messed pretty hard," added Hammond.

"There are a *lot* of angry demons under our feet," Drusilla said, looking down.

"Right you are, love. Let's not be under theirs when they start finding their way up." Spike cleared his throat. "Although I do expect some of them are gonna be in better shape than others. That blighter Sisseroth took an otter through the head. Gonna take him a long time to Humpty Dumpty all those bits back into the right shapes."

"I think it was a badger," said Drusilla. "Not an otter."

"I think it was effective," said Spike.

Rieka ignored them both and kept digging.

"Mm?" Drusilla lifted Ed's doll to her head. "Yes. Yes. We're getting to you. Wait your turn."

"You know she can't actually speak to you?" Hammond began.

"Don't worry about it," said Spike. "That's our cue. Come on, love. Let's make like that barkeep in Madrid and crawl away, bleeding."

They began to gradually pick their way down the mountain of debris. The worst of it had finally settled, and the air had cleared to the color of weak tea. Spike glanced around as they made their wobbly descent. The tower had collapsed onto the rest of the house, reducing the entire property to an expensive hill of broken boards and cracked bricks.

A set of dusty fingers reached up from the debris ahead of Spike, feebly attempting to push aside a lump of granite the size of a bathtub. Spike strongly considered pretending he hadn't seen them—they were so nearly done with this nightmare of a failed heist—but something gave him pause. He carefully made his way to the struggling hand and knelt for a closer look. His ribs ached from the movement, but he brushed a layer of dust off the fumbling fingers, which startled at his touch. The skin beneath was a pale purple.

"That you, mate?" Spike asked.

All sound around them ceased for a few seconds and then returned.

"You could just say *yes*, you show-off." Spike stood and waved Rieka and Hammond over. Soon, the four of them had shifted away enough rubble to pull Ermack out. He looked like he had spent the night doing somersaults in a rock quarry, but with a bit of help, he could walk.

They helped him over the shifting wreckage and onto solid ground, and then Rieka took over, escorting him down to the dusty street.

"Aw, would you look at those two." Drusilla leaned into Spike as they watched the demon and werewolf fade away into the London fog.

"I see them," said Spike. "I see a pair of vile monsters who would have cheerfully buried all of London alive if it got them their own personal happily ever after."

"Exactly." Drusilla sighed. "They remind me of us."

"I was thinking the same thing," Spike said.

"You two are a pair." Hammond chuckled. "Promise you'll get Ed sorted before you go?"

"We'll see to her," Spike said. "And then I'll see about collecting our fee—and Mucker's fee, too, while we're at it." He winced as his ribs tightened. The punctured lung was knitting itself back together. He hated that feeling. "Although maybe our payday trip can wait a night or two."

"You'll get what you're owed," Hammond assured him. And then, with a nod, he made off down an alley and away, vanishing into the night.

Drusilla and Spike made their way back toward the carriage house across the street. A gas lamp, which had been snapped at the base like a broken matchstick, lay across the sidewalk, quietly venting fumes into the air. The two of them stepped over it. All along the street, windows were aglow, concerned faces pressed against the glass to try to see the source of all the commotion.

"Yes, I heard you the first time," Drusilla chided the doll. The doll remained inanimate and unresponsive. "We're almost there."

"Actually"—as they neared the carriage house, Spike pulled Drusilla aside—"give me a moment first, would you?"

Drusilla shrugged and leaned against a brick arch to wait.

Spike slipped into the building and made his way back to the carriage where they had left their immobilized accomplice. "Break time's over, Ed," he said, opening the door. Her body remained on the seat, placid and peaceful as ever, in spite of the devastation that had taken place across the lane.

"It's about time," Ed said, her eyelids fluttering half open. "Well? Tell Drusilla to bring me back to my body at once. I know she's right outside."

"Soon," said Spike evenly. "Tell me about Mucker first."

Ed hesitated, her lips pursed. "He . . . betrayed you," she said at last. "He betrayed all of us. Now stop playing around and let me get back into my body."

"He said *we needed a couple of patsies*," Spike pressed. "*We.* Not I. So somebody else was in on the double-cross. I'd like to know who. Tell me the truth."

"I *am* telling you the truth, you babbling idiot," she insisted. "Now go tell Drusilla to get over here. What is she doing waiting by the—" Ed's mouth opened wide, and she let out a gasp. "Oh no!"

From behind Spike came the sudden banging of a door and the clump of footsteps. Spike pulled his head out of the carriage just as a wicked metallic blade carved through the door's hinges like they were made of sculpting clay. The door made a momentary squeal of protest and then thudded to the ground at Spike's feet.

Spike blinked up at the Dread Lord of London Town.

Gunnar was panting like an angry bull, his silk shirt hanging in tatters off of his gargantuan frame. He allowed the tip of the demonic spear to scrape along the ground as he took slow steps forward. The carriage house, which had housed the entire crew so comfortably, felt suddenly crowded.

"Oh," said Spike. "Belphegor's bollocks."

CHAPTER TWENTY-FIVE

he hulking shape of the angry Hastam demon blocked Spike's path to the exit. With the flick of his wrist, Gunnar's demonic spear could cut Spike in half. "You thought you could destroy my house," Gunnar snarled, "and I'd just let you walk away?"

"Well, that wasn't the original plan," Spike countered. "But now that you mention it, that would be dandy if—" Before he could finish, Gunnar roared and swung the blade.

Spike dove into the carriage to avoid the strike. He rolled over Ed's lap and slammed into the opposite door, righting himself clumsily as he fumbled with the handle.

"What's happening?" Ed demanded. "Your useless girlfriend isn't even pointing me toward the carriage house. Spike? Oh, you're worthless, both of you! I'm glad I sold you out! I would do it again! Master Gunnar? Are you there? I did everything you asked. I can't see what's—"

And then Ed's voice abruptly stopped.

The door finally opened, and Spike tumbled through it. He hit the ground on the opposite side before looking back.

Gunnar's blade had skewered Ed straight through her chest, pinning her already-lifeless body to the seat. Gunnar withdrew the wicked lance, then snarled and lashed out again, carving a gash clear through the carriage roof—and lopping Ed's head off her body in the process.

Spike gulped. That was two of his new associates decapitated in one night. Spike didn't fancy becoming number three. He clambered to his feet and backed up until he was pressed against the wall of the building. Gunnar stomped around the back of the carriage.

"Look," Spike tried. "You seem like a reasonable monster." He edged past the front wheels as Gunnar circled, keeping the carriage between himself and the furious demon.

"I'm gonna break every bone in your scrawny body," Gunnar growled. He planted a hand on the side of the vehicle and shoved, hard. It flipped through the air and punched a carriage-size hole in the wall of the building. Spike suddenly found himself face-to-face with the Hastam demon, nothing between the two of them. "I'm gonna turn your skin into a tablecloth," Gunnar continued. "And *then* I'm gonna kill you."

The blade sliced through the air toward Spike's feet. Spike leaped over the strike and made a mad dash for the gaping hole in the wall. A fist the size of a baked ham caught him in the gut as he vaulted, sending his world spinning. He hit the ground and rolled, stumbling to his feet and then almost immediately tripping over the fallen lamppost. He landed hard on his back as Gunnar stomped out of the ruined carriage house.

Spike rubbed his side. Damn, the guy sure could move for such a hulking titan. He pushed himself up, his hands sliding on the loose bricks and cracked cobblestones beneath him. Clearing his throat, he palmed a few loose stones before drawing himself to his feet. So the demon was a titan. The titans lost their fight, if Spike remembered correctly. This wasn't over yet.

"That all you got?" Spike managed, sounding wheezier than he had intended. "I've fought worse than you. I brought down a slayer, remember?" He pitched a broken cobblestone weakly at the demon.

Gunnar batted the projectile away with his blade effortlessly. The flint sparked against the metallic edge and tinkled to the ground in pieces. Spike's eyes darted from side to side, and he took another step back into the street.

"There's *nothing* worse than me," Gunnar snarled, stalking after him. "In the time it took you to snuff out one snot-nosed child with a pointy stick, I've brought down hundreds of enemies—every one of them more worthy than you. Have you forgotten? I took down an Old One. You? You're *nothing*."

Spike readied a second old cobblestone. The metal lamppost bent under Gunnar's foot as he trod closer. Spike's eardrums must finally have begun to heal, because he could hear the faintest hiss.

"Yeah. Maybe," Spike said. "But I make nothing *work*." He let the shard of flint fly, and again Gunnar batted it away reflexively. This time, however, the resulting spark found fuel in the cloud of gas gushing out of the broken pipe.

The initial burst lit the street like flash powder. Spike covered his eyes. The heat of it was enough to singe the ends of his hair. Even after the first blast, a steady geyser of flame danced merrily in the night.

Spike let out a satisfied sigh and dropped the rest of the stones, wiping his hands on his trousers. By the light of the fire, he could see Drusilla standing just under a brick archway a dozen feet up the road. Her brow was knit, and her gaze was a million miles away.

"That wasn't so hard," panted Spike.

A familiar laugh filled the street.

Spike froze.

Gunnar walked calmly through the fountain of flames, letting the fire lick at his flesh like it was no more than a pleasant breeze. "You don't know anything about Hastam demons, do you?" he chortled.

Spike swallowed. "Not nearly as much as I'd like," he croaked. "Not every monster has Bram bloody Stoker writing entire books about their weaknesses. I take it fire doesn't make the list of yours. Good to know. Don't suppose you'd care to go off on a convenient monologue about what *can* kill you?"

"Not *you*. That's for sure." Gunnar's hand flicked, and the demonic blade pierced through the air faster than Spike could dodge it. Spike let out a groan as the whole right side of his body erupted with pain. For the second time that night, he found himself pierced clean through his torso. He would really appreciate it if this sodding night would lay off his lungs for a little while. He had only just healed the last one. At least, he found himself musing, the holes would balance each other out until they faded.

Gunnar pressed the weapon deeper, letting the metal slide roughly along Spike's ribs as he leaned in. Spike let out a weak grunt as the demon's face drew closer to his.

"Dru?" Spike managed breathlessly. "Little help?"

Drusilla's eyes were wide, and her gaze drifting. "He's coming," she whispered. "And he is angry."

"Thanks," Spike wheezed. "Slightly late on that one."

Gunnar flexed his arm and lifted. With his rib cage thrumming in pain, Spike felt his feet leave the ground. He clutched desperately at the demon's weapon, striving to take some of the weight off his injury. The pain was making him dizzy, but he strained his eyes, trying to focus on Gunnar.

How *did* you stop a Hastam demon? There was always something, some trick, even with the most powerful ones. Fire would have worked on a Lilliad. With the Mohra, you only had to smash that shiny gem in their foreheads. Just about anything could kill a hellhound if you hit them with it hard enough. So what was Gunnar's Achilles' heel?

"What's the matter?" Gunnar teased. "Not quite so talkative all of a sudden?"

"I've made—*ngh*—a decision," Spike wheezed. "I'm gonna—*rrgh*—let you off easy."

Gunnar grinned from ear to crimson ear. The crown of horns around his head glistened in the firelight. "Still cracking wise? Good. I'm going to enjoy breaking you, rat."

"Ugh," Spike groaned. "You dramatic types always take everything—*ngh*—so personally."

"Have you *seen* this mess?" Gunnar nodded at the rubble. "This feels a little personal."

"Oh, come on," Spike grunted. "Big deal. I tried to—*urnf*—steal a teensy-weensy pinkie from you, then *you* tried to trap me forever in a magical torture box, then I broke your house. We could go back and forth like this for—*oogh*—centuries, or we could just call it even."

"Call it *even*?" Gunnar snarled. Beside them, the pile shuddered, and a cracked roofing tile slid down a slope of debris to shatter into pieces on the ground.

"Sure," Spike managed. "I'll let you walk away. Call it a draw. I've never been one to—*grrk*—hold a grudge."

The mountain of wreckage shuddered again, bricks clinking and beams creaking, and this time the whole street rumbled with it. Spike felt the spear dip as Gunnar's eyes narrowed and his attention flicked to the trembling ruins.

"He's *here*," whispered Drusilla.

The remains of Gunnar's mansion rose suddenly, building to an unsteady peak until the detritus burst apart with all the violence of an erupting volcano. Rising from the center was an unearthly vision of gnashing fangs and snapping mandibles—the horrific head of a wormlike monster the size of an express train. Sorm.

Gunnar gaped at the Old One. The monstrous body just kept coming, its rough, thick hide rising from the ruins like billowing smoke. High in the air, a face that had been forged from primordial nightmares turned its golden eyes toward the earth. Numbly, Gunnar retracted the spear from Spike's chest with a sticky *shluck*. Spike gasped and collapsed to the ground.

The Old One slowed, its neck twisting and its body arching several stories above the ground. As the great beast's trajectory turned back toward the earth, those glistening eyes fixed on Gunnar, and a tense energy crackled along the street like the air before a thunderstorm.

"You know"—Spike coughed, dragging himself backward, away from the Hastam demon—"*I* may not hold a grudge. But something tells me your old buddy Sorm *does*."

The Old One's primal roar cut through the quiet night like a brick cuts through jelly. The titan barreled toward the earth like a meteor. Spike rolled out of the way as best he could, his entire body aching. He was no more than ten feet away when the gargantuan maw enveloped Gunnar. The Old One did not stop there. The street buckled under the impact of the wide, wicked jaws, sending ripples of force outward, cracking cobblestones into pieces and splintering flagstones like they were no more than the crust on a delicate Greek pastry.

Spike stared. One moment, Gunnar had been standing in front of him, and the next, a tower of lumpy scales was descending into the earth where the Dread Lord of London Town had been. Rocks began to glow with the heat of the friction as the primordial monster plowed its way downward. The sound—although magnitudes louder—was not unlike the morning train rumbling its way down the Twopenny Tube. In another few moments, the last tip of the primordial terror's tail had thundered away beneath the surface. The trembling did not stop, but it faded gradually, like the steady aftershocks of an earthquake.

"Huh," Spike managed eloquently.

The scene swayed in front of his eyes. He could tell without getting too close that the hole the creature had left behind was unfathomably deep. The sounds echoing up from below might have been a mile away already. A few bricks, chunks of plaster, and other debris from the demolished tower slid over the lip and made distant clicks and clacks as they tumbled into the void.

Meanwhile, the fire, still fountaining up from the broken gas line, had spread. It had completely engulfed the overturned carriage and climbed beyond it to the already ruined carriage house, devouring the wood with a happy crackling. As Spike watched, flaming embers hopped onto a neighbor's awning and threatened the canvas roof of a vendor's cart parked half a block down the road.

Neighbors gawked from their windows. From up the street, the distant sound of sirens grew louder. In any moment, the place would be crawling with police and fire trucks and ambulances. This was likely to stretch the guild's definition of *keeping a low profile*.

"Are you done playing with your friends, my sweet?" Drusilla's voice called out.

Spike swung his head toward her. "Exceedingly done," he managed. "Let's get out of here."

"You always play so rough." She picked her way toward him. "Did you know the Old One was going to gobble up Gunnar in the end?"

"Sure," he croaked. "All part of the plan."

Drusilla reached an arm out to help Spike to his feet. "You're all bloody," she said, a spark dancing in her eyes. "I like it."

"Good energy, love. Let's save that for later. *Ungh.*" He grimaced as jolts of pain clanged through his body, rattling through organs he hadn't known were still in there. "Much later," he grunted.

The two of them cast one last glance back at the place where the mansion on Wych Street had been. Most of the building had collapsed back into the cavity the serpent had vacated, leaving a hilly crater of rubbish. The arm of an expensive sofa was sticking out of the rubble. Spike could still see the intricate figures carved all along it, but it was so caked in dust he could scarcely make out who was torturing whom. Once-elegant crystals dangled from a thoroughly mangled chandelier, the prisms swaying limply in the soft breeze. Here and there a shiny gold coin or a glittering gemstone from Gunnar's collection caught the light from within the gravel and garbage—literal diamonds in the rough.

Spike's eyes landed on a small, ashen shape at the foot of an upturned armoire. His breath caught in his throat—which was convenient, as his abused lungs didn't particularly want it at the moment. He stooped down sorely and picked up a small calloused gray finger.

It was warm to the touch.

"Is it?" Drusilla whispered, behind him.

"No." He sighed. "This one's much too fresh. Probably Sisseroth." He tossed the dingy digit back into the pile, his shoulders sagging. "After all this, I still didn't get you that relic," Spike said. "It's probably been ground to dust."

Drusilla's expression clouded glumly, but she nodded and patted Spike's arm. "It's all right, my love."

"But it isn't!" Spike ran a hand through his hair and pulled away. Drusilla watched him as he turned a pained expression to the heavens.

"What are you thinking?" she asked.

"I just . . . Ever since you-know-who skipped out on us, you've been . . . different. More distant." Spike cleared his throat. "The Relic of Saint Agabus is more than some old piece of a prophet. It was supposed to help you get over all that and look to the future—our future." He was having trouble meeting her eyes. "It was gonna keep you from leaving me to go off looking for *him*."

"Oh, sweet Spike," Drusilla said. "I'm not going to go looking for Angelus. I don't need to. He's going to find *us*—even if it takes him a hundred years and he has to march through the valley of the sun. He's going to come back and help us destroy the whole world. I've seen it."

"Hurrah," he said wretchedly.

"You don't want the family to be all together again?" Drusilla said. Her brow furrowed.

"I want to be all the *wicked* that you need, Dru." Spike sighed— or tried to sigh. Most of the air escaped his leaky lungs before it could make it to his throat. "I want to be all you think about. I want to give you the whole world, impaled on the tip of a silver spear." His shoulders drooped. "I couldn't even give you a single sodding finger."

Drusilla's face softened. "Oh, my lovely Spike."

"I'll get you other fingers, if you want. Fresh fingers. Tonight!"

"It's not about how wicked you are," she said, "or about how many fingers you rip off of some pretty young victim down by the pier. It's about being wicked and ripping off fingers *together*."

Spike felt light-headed. "Wait, if you weren't planning on leaving . . ." he managed. "It was never your ticket, was it?"

Drusilla looked confused.

"Forget it," said Spike. "I'm a damned fool."

"That's one of my favorite things about you."

His lips stretched into a wobbly smile. "I don't deserve you."

"You know I love it when people say that to me, *especially* when they're all covered in blood," she said. She leaned in close until her nose brushed his, ever so gently. Her hair smelled like warm cloves and sweet cruelty. "But I like it best when *you* say it," she breathed.

"Just to be clear," he whispered, "we *are* gonna go find someone and rip their fingers off for a bit of fun after this, yes?"

"Of course we are," she said. "Together."

And then she kissed him, deeply, passionately. While the myriad aches across Spike's body did not fade away as he embraced her, they did sharpen into something truly exquisite.

CHAPTER TWENTY-SIX

When Drusilla finally pulled herself away, Spike's head was swimming. "Let's go home, Dru."

"I almost forgot," Drusilla said, spinning around. "We can't leave Miss Edith."

Spike drew a breath through his teeth and glanced over at the ever-growing fire that was now happily gobbling up the last of the carriage house and climbing the roof of the building behind it. Smoldering on the paving stones right in front was a charred frame that had once been an overturned carriage.

"Between the impaling, the decapitation, and the incineration," he said, "I'm pretty sure Ed's not coming back. Sorry, love. If it makes you feel any better, she most definitely sold us out to a psychopath before she went." But Drusilla was already on the other side of the street. She knelt near a pile of damp leaves and retrieved the discarded baby doll.

"Oh," said Spike. "That thing. I think that's well and truly just a doll now, Dru. There's no way Ed's in there anymore. Ed's dead."

"Mm?" Drusilla dusted a twig off of the pretty pink dress. "Oh, I suppose. But no sugar lumps for you." It took a moment for Spike to realize she was addressing the doll and not him. She bipped it on the nose with her forefinger. "You heard me. You know what you did. Miss Edith has been much too naughty for sugar lumps."

With Spike's arm around Drusilla's shoulder, the two of them made their way down a slim path between the nearest buildings—the nearest ones that weren't either rubble or actively burning—and Drusilla spotted a sewer grate halfway down the alley. Spike leaned against the wall as she opened it.

A shiny steam pumper rattled past the mouth of the alley, and a police officer on horseback clopped by moments later. Wych Street was rapidly becoming a very crowded lane. Spike winced as he pushed himself off the wall.

Moving quickly was not an option, and explaining themselves to a bevy of authorities was equally out of the question. Drusilla could probably finish most of them off on her own, if it came down to it—and Spike *would* enjoy the spectacle—but the gruesome deaths of scores of men in uniform would only bring more men in uniform, and eventually the guild would notice. Spike didn't want to be exiled. Not yet. He liked London. Retreat, then.

He eased himself onto the ladder after Drusilla, pausing to pull the grate back in place. Just as he lowered it over his head, a woman turned into the alley in front of him. He hesitated. Was she watching him? The flickering firelight lit her from behind and made it hard to tell. She turned her head as heavy footsteps approached, and Spike caught a flash of green behind her ear. A hairpin? No. A pencil.

A man in uniform came into view beside the woman, and

Spike dropped out of sight. The grate clinked shut above him, and he slid stiffly off the ladder.

He listened intently as Drusilla led him beneath the streets. Above them, he could hear the policeman's voice.

"That's right, ma'am. We've had a suspicious report. So, did you see two people fleeing this way? Male and a female?"

"I—I did," the woman answered. "Did *they* do all this?"

"Couldn't say," the cop's voice answered. "Wanted for questioning, though. Which way did they go?"

There was a pause. "Through the alley. Out the other side. They ran off up Holywell Street, I think."

"Thank you, ma'am."

The sound of footsteps clomped away.

As they made their way through the labyrinth of tunnels snaking under London, Spike found himself thinking about old gods who led hunting parties and stags that got away. He wondered if the stag enjoyed the hunt, too. He reasoned that it must, at the very least, enjoy always getting away in the end.

Darla looked down at the scrap of paper in her hand and read, for the third time, the address written in her own fine, tight cursive. Then she looked back up at the flaming chaos that was Wych Street. Darla blinked.

Two gleaming steam pumpers were attempting to put out a blaze that had begun crawling its way up the side of an inn, men in uniforms were stringing a cordon rope around a gaping hole in the road, and there was a mountain of debris right where the Hastam demon's building should be. The neighborhood looked like a wide, angry grimace with one missing tooth.

"Huh," managed Darla.

It had taken her the better part of the evening just to track down the address. She had spoken to five vampires, two demons, a witch, and a bridge troll before procuring it. Then she had rehearsed her introduction the entire way over—carefully finding the perfect balance between flattery and self-confidence to begin her diplomatic meeting on precisely the right foot. Negotiations of this nature required a certain savoir faire, after all.

A chunk of the street gave way and toppled into the hole, tugging the policemen's rope down with it, yard by unraveling yard.

Darla shook her head, watching from the far end of the block as men darted about like frantic little mice with their tails on fire.

A movement to her right caught Darla's attention, and she turned to see a short, skinny figure, a pair of ram's horns poking out of his hair, limping away from all the hubbub. He had the gray remains of a badly torn jacket hanging off his shoulders, and the bony tip of one of his horns had snapped off.

"What happened here?" Darla asked him.

The demon flinched at the sight of her and then glanced nervously behind him.

"Well?"

"Not here," the demon muttered, and gestured for her to follow him around a corner into a more private alleyway. She obliged, warily.

"Look—the thing is," the demon bleated, "we had a good run. But all this is above my pay grade. Without Gunnar—"

"Gunnar is gone? Why didn't you go with him?"

"Because where he went is inside the belly of the hellworm," the demon managed, his voice cracking slightly. "And I would like very much to be as far from here as possible when it comes back for seconds."

"It was you idiots who messed with Sorm?" Darla shook her head, impressed. "Where are you going to go?"

"Away. Out. Back to the old horde. Nobody wants to stick around and find out what the inside of an Old One looks like."

In the shadows beside them, a sewer grate rattled and then flipped open with a resounding *clang*. The demon looked like he might faint but managed to keep his knees from giving out long enough to scurry away into the darkness. From out of the sewer, a figure burst into the night. She was clad in a bloodred dress, black hair whipping behind her as she spun to a landing.

"Elita?" said Darla. "What are *you* doing here?"

Elita straightened. "I have uncovered the cretinous villain behind the capture of Sorm. You will be shocked to learn that the culprit was none other than a demon called—"

"Gunnar. Yeah," said Darla. "I worked that out myself, as it turns out. Very recently."

"Have you come to fight by my side, then, sister? I had thought myself to be the chosen one, but perhaps we two—heirs of the glorious Archaeus bloodline—are destined to be the salvation of Sorm together."

"Oh. Sorry," said Darla. "I know how much you were looking forward to doing something exceedingly stupid tonight, but I'm afraid you just missed him, actually. He seems properly chuffed to be out, if that makes you feel any better. His former captors are pissing themselves."

"Sorm is saved?" Elita stepped around the corner and froze, taking in the carnage. "You?" she demanded.

Darla shook her head.

"This cannot be. It should have been one of our kin."

Darla came to stand at her shoulder as they watched the absolute bedlam playing out on Wych Street. "Oh," said Darla, "I have a feeling it was."

They stood in silence for a minute, the warm, smoky breeze washing over them in gentle waves.

"What will you do now?" Darla asked at last.

"I will rejoin the Order." Elita sounded deflated but resolute. "The Master will be pleased that the matter is resolved, at least. And you? Are you ready to return to him as well?"

Darla opened her mouth but then hesitated.

With Gunnar gone, that building wasn't the only thing that had collapsed—the whole demon syndicate had been suddenly and effectively disbanded. With the demons out of the picture, Blackhearth could ease off on their assault, and an armistice with Blackhearth meant that the Vampires' Guild would accept Drusilla under their full protection. Darla's head felt oddly light. With her family's future looking just a little brighter . . .

"Yes," she said numbly. "I think I might finally be ready to go."

CHAPTER TWENTY-SEVEN

s there really a demonic ghost trapped inside that thing?" Darla
asked Spike later that night as they watched Drusilla wipe cobwebs off the old tea service and set a chipped cup and saucer
daintily in front of the motionless doll.

The figure continued to stare blankly into the middle distance
through its painted eyes.

"I don't . . . think so?" Spike whispered. "Ed *is* dead. Very
dead. I checked."

Across the room, Drusilla poured an amber liquid into the teacups and then laughed airily at something the doll most definitely
had *not* said.

"Yeah. I don't love it," Darla said. "It's creepy."

"Agreed," said Spike. "It's awful, but it makes Dru happy for
now, so I suppose we'll get used to it."

"How appropriate." Darla nodded. "That is precisely what
Angelus and I said about *you* when you first joined up."

Spike allowed himself a smile. "Careful, now. That was almost a compliment."

Darla shrugged. "You *do*, you know," she said softly. "Make her happy."

Spike tore his eyes away from the tea party and raised an eyebrow. "You're being uncharacteristically less than awful. Are we just waiting until Dru brings out the crumpets before you tear into me for the mess I got us into? I brought down a building, remember. There was fire. Loads of witnesses. Brick bits blasted all the way out to the Thames."

"That does ring a bell," Darla said.

"Not anymore, it doesn't," Spike said. "Flattened that thing out like a bronze pancake. Too bad, too. Could've had some fun with it." He rubbed his neck.

"I spoke to Lord Ruthven at the guild already," said Darla. "He said he'll be busy for months making the necessary excuses to the human authorities and helping cover up all the occult activity and demolished architecture. Blackhearth operatives are all over the scene already, confiscating anything interesting that the response crews pull out of the ruins. The whole fiasco is a public-relations nightmare."

"That whinging ninny," Spike scoffed. "Blame a burst gas line like usual and be done with it. He can say that the fumes caused mass hallucinations and then a spark caused the explosion. Boom. Done. Those fool things are going off like Roman candles all the time, anyway—the public will eat it up. Really, do I need to do his job for him?"

"Oh, I do believe he has already come up with something very similar as the preliminary response." Darla nodded. "But it's a bit more complicated than that. Apparently Gunnar carved out a special prison to house that Old One."

"Sorm. Yeah. I saw it. It was in the basement."

"Did you notice that Sorm's prison stretched beneath the entire block and halfway through the neighborhood to the south? The occult enchantments Gunnar had on the whole enclosure were enough to support the buildings above it—but those charms are ruptured now. They're failing fast. A lot more buildings are going to start coming down, and soon. They're all basically sitting on a cracking shell."

"Gunnar gets credit for those," said Spike hastily. "I only did the tower."

"Ruthven's already submitted a viable pretext to Lord Salisbury. Public works. Something about demolishing old slums to make room for modern traffic—widening the roads for the general good, that sort of thing. Apparently streets in the area have been, *ahem*, getting rather backed up lately."

"Particularly when people go throwing rolltop desks into the middle of key thoroughfares, I imagine." He gave her a nod of respect. "The headlines will be all about taxes and traffic, just as Ruthven likes it, then. I suppose he and his guild ghouls will still be hand-delivering me to Blackhearth for execution as soon as they've got their public-relations mess all sorted?"

"I don't think you need to worry about the guild." Darla turned back to watching Drusilla clink glasses with an inanimate toy. "Not to say you haven't made plenty of *other* enemies who would be more than happy to see you leave, but the guild should have your back. Count Orlok, especially—and that is one powerful favor."

"Lord below, I forgot about Orlok."

Darla sighed. "He's talking about you two as if you're his own personal guardian fallen angels."

"Honestly?" said Spike "We didn't even see the blighter in there. I would've bet money that the cowardly cur had run off somewhere to lie low, until he climbed out of the ruins in front of us."

"Yes, well, *he* seems to be under the impression that you two, as devoted guild loyalists, orchestrated the whole daring attack on his behalf, and for the good of all London vampires." She shrugged. "Clearly he's never spent any length of time with you. But I didn't rush to correct him. To hear him explain it, you're some unholy Robin Hood. The vampire community had all but lost their hold on the London underworld, but with Gunnar and all of his top operatives out of commission, the whole syndicate is falling apart. The demon population is already splintering into more manageable factions again."

"I did that?"

"More than that. You didn't hear it from me, but it seems Blackhearth is anticipating a steep and sudden decline in demonic activity in London, and they are crediting the guild for assisting in that effort as temporary allies. Boats drifting through the same waters and all that. I doubt they had any more idea than we did how to stamp out a Hastam demon, and you've managed to do their job for them. As such, Buckingham's best have consented to direct their resources elsewhere for a while. No more daylight Blackhearth raids on vampire nests. Lord Ruthven is looking forward to hosting Darkmarket."

"Are you saying," said Spike, "that I'm some sort of bloody hero?"

"You and I both know I would *never* use that exact word to

describe you." Darla shook her head. "But there *was* some talk of gratitude from the larger undead community. Ridiculous, I know, but Ruthven informed me that our request for more suitable housing will be expedited as a result—so who was I to argue? You can move Drusilla out of that hovel and into a nice respectable former crime scene. Not a moment too soon, either—I'm pretty sure that lumpy green thing growing on the wall in the back room ate one of the rats."

"Wow. The whole vampire community is in *my* debt?" Spike blinked. "Well then. Who's the impulsive idiot now?"

"Definitely still you. One hundred percent you," said Darla. She considered for a moment. "But maybe that's not *such* a bad thing."

"No?"

Darla grudgingly nodded. "There's a fire in you."

"Is there?" Spike said. "That might explain why everything still hurts."

"You know what I mean. Angelus had a fire, too. It's the reason I chose him, so many years ago. He burned so hot in the beginning; I could feel his heat stoking the embers in me. You do that for Drusilla, too. After nearly three hundred years, I suppose I sometimes forget how good that heat can feel."

"You don't look a day over two hundred and fifty," Spike assured her.

"Stop prattling on when I'm trying to be less than awful to you. Where was I?"

"You were saying I'm impatient," said Spike, "and also on fire."

"Right. It's true. You make asinine decisions and countless mistakes."

"I'm blushing. Go on."

"But do you know what else you do? You *accomplish* things— things other vampires would never even attempt. You really do make *nothing* work. You've been a creature of darkness for all of twenty years, and already you've taken down a slayer and toppled the most powerful demon in England. You just don't know when to stop. So . . . you *don't*. What's next? Take over as a new guild chancellor? With Claudia and Varney gone, they'll still need to fill the seats. The convention is only a few weeks away, and you could almost certainly secure the votes."

"Spend all day with those tossers?" Spike grimaced. "Definitely not. I'd end up smelling like cabbage."

"I thought you'd say something like that. What will you do, then? Are you going to go fill the void in the London underworld and take over where that nasty Hastam left off? I'm beginning to believe you could do it."

"What? *Spike: Dread Lord of London Town*, you mean?"

"The king is dead," Darla replied. "Long live the king."

"Nah." Spike shook his head. "I'd be bored to bleeding playing king-of-the-mountain all the time, sitting on my throne barking orders, always looking over my shoulder. Let some other pretentious plonkers claw their way into the position."

"What, then?"

Spike shrugged and cleared his throat. "Hammond and his crew were talking about maybe joining Mad McElroy on a good old-fashioned slice and heist in a few weeks. They might still need some muscle. Dunno. Sounded like it could be a bit of fun."

Darla regarded him. "You surprise me."

"I'm *full* of surprises," he said. "And also fire, apparently. And definitely some loose gravel. It's been a rough few days."

"So you really wouldn't want to rule London with an iron fist if you had the chance? Ever since we came back from China, it seems like all you've wanted was to be a god among monsters. What changed?"

"I'm already a god among monsters, love. Maybe I just decided I want to be the sort of god who goes on hunts and carries his own spear into battle instead of sitting idly on a throne." Spike leaned his back against the crumbling wall. "I don't need a fancy mansion like Gunnar's," he said, "or a bunch of soft-headed cretins throwing themselves at my feet. And it's never been about polishing my trophies. Maybe I got caught up in all that for a minute—but that's not me. It's about the thrill of the chase." They watched Drusilla fastidiously straightening the table settings. "And most of all, it's about who's there with me."

Darla bit her lip. "Speaking of which . . ." she began.

"I know the ticket was yours," said Spike. "It's okay. You don't need to worry about Dru. I'll look after her. That's a promise." He met Darla's eyes. "And I keep my promises."

Darla nodded. "I believe you."

"When do you leave?"

"Soon."

From across the room, Drusilla turned toward the two of them expectantly.

"But first," Darla whispered, "I think it's about time for tea."

Spike nodded. "We may be abominations," he said, "but we are *English* abominations."

CHAPTER TWENTY-EIGHT

T he woman was worried, Spike could tell. He watched silently as she crossed the street, a gas lamp flickering warmly behind her and a gentle breeze rolling off the Thames. She was right to be worried. In the distance, church bells rang out the hour. Midnight. The woman looked to her left and right before taking a seat on an iron bench overlooking the water. Her foot tapped nervously against the flagstones. In her arms was a leather portfolio. She hugged it tightly.

Spike slipped out of the shadows and stalked toward her, savoring the approach. His chest was still tight—it probably would be for weeks—but his injuries had already had several days to heal, and they were coming along nicely, all things considered. The process had been helped in no small part by Spike's being treated to a seemingly bottomless sampling of fresh blood from the finest guild victims. His favorite of the bunch had been a full-bodied O positive, imported from some quiet spot in France—but he would have sooner taken another spear to the chest than admit as much to Lord Ruthven.

The woman started with an audible gasp as Spike dropped onto the bench beside her. He said nothing at first, simply sat there, watching the boats bob on the river. He listened to her pulse speed up, and he smiled. Her fear was delicious.

"Still carrying your monster manuscript all over London at all hours of the night?" he asked conversationally, nodding at the portfolio.

Miss Eriksson looked down. "This?" She hesitated. "This is a new story, actually. Just a project I started in my spare time. I'm trying something . . . different."

"Well, you're writing. And you look well. Good enough to eat, in fact."

"I *am* writing," she said hurriedly. "Professionally writing. For money, I mean—do you believe it?"

Spike looked impressed. "You sold that anachronistic drivel? Good for you."

She looked down at her toes. "Not that one, no. An article. For the *Gazette*. They haven't exactly promoted me to a real writing position yet, but I penned my first news story a few days ago and they bought it! For real money! Not a lot, but my editor says they always need more material, as long as the writing's up to snuff."

"Mm." Spike made a face. "Journalism. Well, better you than me."

"The funny thing is," she said, her eyes rising to meet his, "I had finally put away all my frivolous ideas about evil monsters and occult dangers and decided to try my hand at writing a serious news story. I followed a lead, even interviewed a few perfectly normal witnesses about a perfectly normal gas leak—and what do you suppose those people wanted to talk to me about?"

Spike might have paled, if he wasn't at maximum pale already. "Your first article—the one you published for all London to read—was about the Wych Street incident?"

She nodded. "Curious how many people seem to have seen the same, erm, hallucination. Their descriptions were very . . . *specific*."

Spike narrowed his eyes. "Descriptions of what, exactly?"

"Don't worry," she said, letting her eyes drop again. "Nothing that one might consider *frivolous* made it into print."

Spike looked at her for several seconds. "Hang on," he said. "You *know*? You know what I *am*?" It was a good thing Spike had already made plans to dump Miss Eriksson's remains in the Thames at the end of this meeting. Things were finally looking up, and he did not need some nosy human mucking it all up for him all over again.

Miss Eriksson did not answer right away. She bit her lip nervously and slid the leather folder across the bench. Spike glanced from it to the woman and back again.

"My new project," she said. "The first chapter, anyway. I took some advice from a friend. It's set right here in England, this time. Modern London vampire. Debonair chap. Good cheekbones."

Spike picked up the manuscript mutely. He opened the portfolio and riffled through a few pages. "You forgot *great hair*," he said at last.

Miss Eriksson swallowed. "Think you might be willing to give me some suggestions?" she asked. "I want to get it right. Maybe it could be even *better* than *Dracula*?"

Spike turned pages slowly, his lips tight as he scanned the text.

"If you know what I am," he said, "then you know I wasn't kidding. What if I decide to murder you horribly at any moment?"

"I asked myself that very thing," she said.

"And?"

"And then I asked myself: What if he *doesn't*?"

Spike's lips twitched up in a grin, his eyes still on the page. "I may have a few notes," he said.

END

ACKNOWLEDGMENTS

So many brilliant artists have collaborated to create the world of *Buffy the Vampire Slayer* and turn it into a paranormal playground for countless fans over the years. I cannot fully express the joy I have felt being invited to add my own story to this universe, and I'm so grateful to all of the creative minds that came before me to build these supernatural structures. This book would not exist, of course, without the incredibly talented James Marsters, Juliet Landau, and Julie Benz, who each brought such vibrant life to their respective undead darlings. Like so many fans, I can't help but love these wonderfully wicked characters from eyeballs to entrails.

Thanks to Lucy for being *almost* as excited about this project as I have been, to Preeti for being a sounding board when I needed one, to Ben for diving into impromptu discussions about naughty British words, and—as always—to Katrina for countless hours of support and suggestions along the way. I'm also so grateful for all the *BtVS* fans, collectives, and podcasts out there, still sharing memes, quotes, and deep thoughts about this amazing universe. (I see you, *Slayerfest98*.) It has been a joy to dive back into this community and a delight to be reminded of the myriad ways that the show continues to inspire and empower fans from so many walks of life. Stay sharp and keep slaying, everybody!